FROM S

FROM SEA TO SHINING SEA

FROM SEA TO SHINING SEA

...AGAINST THE GRAIN, A THRILLER.

MIKE MAHAR

Tidewatcher Press

Wells, New York and Lahinch, Ireland

From Sea to Shining Sea

This book is dedicated to Charles P. Mahar
Youngest of 9, Provider, Romantic, Marine, Policeman, Author, Father,
and so much more.
R.I.P.

Contents

1

Prologue

The blond secretary with the beehive points her pencil at the closed door.

"Mr. Mann?" Her voice startles me. "Mr. Mullens can see you now."

I hesitate an instant, lost in my worries. Then the cheap paneling and faux leather, the neon office lights and the click-clack of typewriters bring me back to my sorry mission. I clench my jaw and stand. It's taken a lot to get me to this point, and even so I'm still uncomfortable with my decision. I'm conscious of the tension and try to relax. Doing what I'm about to do intimidates and terrifies me. So does Mitch Mullens. My divorce lawyer. Mitch is standing behind his desk. He's a head shorter than my six feet, probably forty pounds heavier than my one eighty. His expensive suit doesn't fit well. Neither does the smile on his pasty face.

"Hey, John, nice day. They treating you well over in the Valley?"

"Can't complain, Mitch." We shake, my hand moist, his cold and lifeless. Mitch and I were in High School together, never friends, but he's the only divorce lawyer I know. "How about you?"

"Doing great." Mitch sits down and spreads his hands. "Look, I've got to get out of the office a little early today, in a foursome with the mayor, so do you mind if we get into it?"

"Sooner the better," I say with an unexpected sigh. "I've reached my limit."

"That bad, is it?" Mitch is at his desk, the recently added monitor takes up a whole corner of the oak monstrosity. Behind him row atop row of leather bound tomes and a pin dot printer. I cross my legs, conscious of my blue jeans and sandals. The second floor office is in a residential area, the hum of traffic can be heard through the windows.

"I've got your paperwork here." Mitch's pate reflects a sheen of sweat as his chubby fingers snake through the files. The window air conditioner rattles and rumbles, no match for the southern California summer. Phones shrill in the outer office. Someone's pager goes off. Mitch holds up a file, triumphant smirk on his face.

"Does Jennifer suspect anything?" he asks.

"No," I say, and then surprise myself. "I really don't like keeping this from her, surprising her, hurting her."

"She's left you no choice, John." Mitch stops rifling through the stack of papers and looks up at me. "From what you've told me she barely takes a sober breath these days. You can't talk things out with someone like that. Or let them raise your daughter."

I feel my gut wrench. He's hit me in the soft spot, again. I never wanted this. Jen and I wanted so much more.

"Bad last night. I had to work late. Little Susan wasn't fed or washed when I came in. Jenny was drunk, chased me around the house, screaming ridiculous things, things I can't make sense of." I was suddenly breathless, gulped some air. "I don't know what else to do. I've got to get Susan out of there. I have to get out of there." Mitch purses his lips, looks almost concerned.

"Sure, John."

"Then maybe Jenny can get some help. If this patent goes through I'll be able to pay for treatment." Mitch's head snaps up, his birdlike eyes focused on me for the first time.

"No patent until the divorce is settled." Now he does look concerned, and points his finger at me. "Don't you even let on that a financial windfall might be in the works. We've agreed on that strategy John, don't blow it now. We've got enough paperwork to sink her in court." He drops his hand and tries a smile. "What you're offering is more than generous under the circumstances, especially since you're also suing for full custody of Sharon."

"Susan."

"What? Oh, yeah, Susan. After the legal stuff is all settled, and you've paid my fee, you can do whatever you want."

I don't like his smile as he turns the papers to face me and pushes them across the desk. My heart sinks, but still I take the black desk pen from its plastic base and sign where the yellow sticky arrows tell me.

"I'll drop these off at the courthouse on my way to the club. Don't tip her off. She'll be served in a day or two. Best for you to stay scarce. Is there anyone can watch Sharon for a while?"

"Susan. No. Jenny only has an Uncle, both of our parents are dead. I have a sister in New York, but she doesn't know about any of this." Mitch closes the file and stands up.

"OK, then, I guess we're all done here. Time for the wheels of justice to start grinding away." He winks at his secretary as we walk to the elevator. We part on the sidewalk. He doesn't return my wave. I figure in his head he's already on the first tee kissing the mayor's ass.

2

Eight Years On, Albany, New York

I feel a tremor in my hand as the cell phone touches my ear. I don't have to get involved, I just have to tell them. The body on the macadam is about fifty feet away. Two rings. Still I hesitate, but feel forced to speak.

"I'm John Mann. I just saw a man shot."

The 911 operator's questions are to the point.

"Behind the New York State Museum, in the private parking lot."

I leave the protection and the shade of the small glade, the coolness of the landscape feature replaced by the suns rays and the heat rolling off the tarmac.

She asks the condition of the victim.

The eyes have clouded over, a look of disbelief lingers. Arms and legs are splayed. A life's work of observation and transport finished.

"He's dead." Standing over the body my voice sounds far away. "Shot through the heart." A question about the living.

"He ran along the side of the Museum, toward Madison Avenue." The dispatcher promises help is on the way, asks me to stay put. Stay put? Am I ready to deal with this? With police?

"I will."

Don't overthink this. I'm just a citizen doing my duty. That's all. I look at the victim. The man lay on his back with blood leaking out under him. About my height, a little heavier, well dressed, a professional man. African American, while I'm Caucasian. Dead, while I'm alive.

I hear sirens. The late summer afternoon's peace is over. The heat of the day starts to ebb as a soft breeze lifts the leaves of the poplar trees sprinkled around the secluded parking area. My sweat soaked shirt begins to cool, but that's not what causes the shiver. The Capitol Police arrive first, two cars. The Albany Police are a heartbeat behind. Three cars. One State Police cruiser, doesn't stay long. A bright red Hook and Ladder next, two paramedics jump off, get a nod from the cops, and hurry to the side of the man. I step back to give them room.

It appears the gig belongs to the Albany Police. The sergeant, portly but fit, red face showing the years, gait the miles, walks up to me, calm down body language but quick eyes.

"You called 911."

"Yes. I saw him get shot," I nod at the figure on the ground. The cop raises his eyebrows, wants more. "I was jogging over in the park. I stopped to catch my breath there, in those trees. I heard someone say something, and when I looked I saw the two men standing here."

No need to mention the noise, the pink spray or dark red liquid where the bullet fought through flesh, bone, organ and tailored suit. I don't mention the crippling fear, I don't tell him that I'd dropped to my knees so the man wouldn't see me.

"What happened next, sir?" There's urgency in the sergeant's voice.

"I heard a shot. I saw the wound in his back. He fell, hit the ground and didn't move. The guy that shot him took his watch and wallet. His briefcase. He ran off that way."

I point at a route that goes alongside the immense Museum building, well maintained paths weaving through the manicured landscape. The afternoon sunlight glints off the distant cars on Madison Avenue, and beyond it the Empire State Plaza, crowded with office workers and tourists. The sergeant turns away and speaks into a device attached to his jacket. Turns back.

"Can you describe the assailant?"

I take a breath and close my eyes. I see him. I look up at the cop.

"Short, stocky, black hair, cut close. Jeans, I think. Short sleeved shirt. Dark. Not tucked in. He put the gun in his waistband."

"Caucasian, African American, Hispanic, Asian?"

"He was white."

The sergeant turns again to the device on his jacket. Turns back.

"Did either man say anything?"

"The shooter. That's what got my attention. He called a name. Dixon."

This time the device calls the sergeant.

"Please wait here."

The police vehicles have their lights flashing, but its late afternoon and there aren't many onlookers. Officers keep the few gawkers at a distance. Several vehicles dot the lot, unhappy owners denied access. One of the cars probably belongs to the corpse at my feet.

"I'll tell Fendrick," I hear the sergeant say.

The fire department paramedics are leaving, a yellow jumpered fireman directing the hook and ladder as it reverses out, the shrill intermittent backup noise a crow defending his nest. I envy them their exit. I'm cooling down from the run and can feel the warmth of the sun, but that shiver comes from somewhere the sun can't reach.

I hear car doors slam, and look up. Two men out of a late model Chevrolet. Summer weight sports coats and narrow ties, a little out of shape, probably athletes in their day. Detectives now. They glance at the mound on the pavement, speak with the sergeant and look my way. Like ominous storm clouds they head toward me and show their IDs. One is Fendrick, taller, more worn, the blue veins in his nose bracketed by the bags under his eyes. The other is Callahan, sandy hair thinning, trim, looks like a high school coach. Fendrick asks the same questions as the sergeant and gets the same answers. Callahan takes careful notes, his freckled hand holding the pen tightly. Fendrick pauses, looks at me and tilts his head to one side. He's making a decision, and I'm consumed with dread.

"Mr. Mann, I'd like you to sit with us in our car. We've picked up a suspect; want to know if you can identify him. If not, we'll keep looking. Will you do this for us?"

We walk to the Chevy. I feel lightheaded as I get in the back seat, the air close, plastic hot on my legs and back. A state police cruiser pulls up in front of us. The driver gets out and stands by, hand on holstered gun. One of the local cops walks to the back door, looks at the trooper, gets a nod and opens it. A handcuffed man stumbles out, the cop protecting his head.

The cop walks the guy around, turns him in different directions, giving me every opportunity to view him. I feel I'm falling down a rabbit hole. Fendrick turns in his seat to face me, brow furrowed, grey eyes doubtful. "Well?"

I take a breath. "That's him"

* * *

"Have a seat Mr. Mann, we have some paperwork to take care of. Can I get you a drink? Coffee?" My tongue is stuck to the roof of my mouth. Being in the station brings back the terror from years before, the day Jenny and Susan died.

"That'd be fine. Thanks."

Callahan goes off to find the promised beverage while Fendrick starts pulling forms from one of the file cabinets on the wall. Opposite is a long window with closed vertical blinds. The rooms beige walls barely contain the four desks and plastic side chairs. The large clock over the door says its already after six. I hold up my cellphone. The tremor is still there.

"Can I make a call to my sister, she'll be worried?"

"As soon as I get a little information. It won't take long."

Callahan returns, the paper cup of dark liquid held away from his body, the rubber soled shoes noiseless on the worn tiles. I take a sip and set it on the desk. It's terrible.

"What's your address Mr. Mann?"

I have to clear my throat.

"I share a house here in the city with my sister." Fendrick frowns, the well lined scowl deepens as I give him the address. "I have a cabin in the Adirondacks. I spend most of my time up there." His eyes narrow. "There's no mail service, so my mail goes to my sister's place." Fendrick looks down, still frowning, nods, and takes down the information.

"Where do you work?"

I pause. "I'm retired. I used to work as a freelance software engineer."

Another frown. "Sort of young to be retired, aren't you?" Callahan has pulled over a chair and is sitting to my side. I have to half turn to answer his question.

"Dumb luck, really. I own a patent, for a while now. It continues to be used, possibly always will be. I get paid when it is. It's enough to be comfortable."

"So, you got a patent and just quit working? That's a little odd, isn't it Mr. Mann? Don't most of you guys keep going, make as much as you can?"

I can't help but swallow, they can't help but notice.

"It was getting to be a bit of a rat race. A lot of pressure, heavy competition." The cops stare at me. "The money was too important to a lot of people. In my opinion." My palms are sweaty. I tell myself I'm the good guy here, doing my duty, just a witness.

"We've been able to identify the victim. One Kenneth Dixon, an investigator with the NYS Department of Agriculture. A Senior Investigator. Did you know him?"

"No," I say.

The two cops exchange a glance.

* * *

"This is more of a formality, but necessary for our investigation, Mr. Mann."

We're in a narrow room with a glass partition along one of the long walls. It feels very close, and I can't control the shiver. Callahan notices, then turns as he switches the lights off. Four men walk into a room on the other side of the glass and turn toward us. A cop directs them to face in different directions, then has each one step forward in turn.

"Well?" Callahan asks as Fendrick looks on. I take another deep breath.

"That's him, number three."

As we leave the line-up room I'm visibly shaking. Callahan takes me into a changing room and starts to rummage through one of the lockers, coming up with some dry running gear and a canvas bag with PBA and the names of various charities written on it.

"Some extra gear. Get out of that wet stuff if you want, then wait outside. We'll print the statement for you to sign. OK?"

"Sure. Thanks."

I change and finally have a chance to call Yvette. She's quick to answer.

"Hi sis."

"John, are you OK?" Shorthand for my mental state. "You haven't been running all this time, have you?"

"No. I couldn't call till now, though. Sorry about that."

"Why? Has something happened?"

"No. Not really. Not to me anyway."

"John. Tell me."

"I stopped in some trees by the museum to catch my breath." I close my eyes. "Yvette, I saw a man murdered."

"Oh no! Are you alright?"

"Yeah, I'm OK, but I've been tied up with the police since then, couldn't call until they got my details and formal statement."

She seemed to think about this. "Why?"

I'm sitting on a long wooden bench in a high ceilinged hallway, floor and walls tiled. My own voice sounds strange in this echo chamber, and I can hear voices coming from places I can't see. I lower mine.

"I don't know. It's a little strange." Or I'm a little strange, remains unsaid. "The man who was killed was an investigator with the Ag Dept. Maybe they knew him."

She lets this pass. "Are you coming home soon?"

"I think so. I have to sign the statement, then I should be through."

"Will they catch the killer?"

"They already have. He didn't know anyone saw him. I called the cops right away, was able to give them a description, and they picked him up."

"You're a witness?"

I wait a beat, "Yeah, why?" but I know why.

"Nothing, I guess."

"I better go. I'll be home soon."

"Be careful love, you know." She sounds so sad. "Bye."

I take a deep breath. When I look up Fendrick is standing a few feet away, looking at me and frowning.

3

Homicide Divison

The plastic table was surrounded by eight folding chairs, although only four were occupied. Fendrick and Callahan, with the murder book and coffee cups, are across from a younger man who sits behind a newish briefcase. There's an unopened bottle of Snapple in front of him. The fourth man is about ten years older than the detectives, better dressed and in better shape. Special Agent John Greene wears a tailored suit and a serious expression. He refuses Callahan's offer of coffee.

"John, you've met Joe Hennessy with the DA's office?" Greene nods at the younger man in the glen plaid suit and vest. "Joe, I asked Agent Greene to join us. The victim was with state law enforcement, so there could be federal jurisdiction." Callahan shifts his attention back to Greene, "We've arrested a suspect, we have an eyewitness. However, there are a couple of anomalies." Greene raises an eyebrow.

"Explain."

"The suspect is Jason Broner. This guy's no virgin, got a sheet from when he was younger, he's thirty five now. A couple of burglaries, some physical stuff, but nothing stronger that's stuck to him. Some time upstate. There are suspicions regarding two homicides, but no arrests, no convictions."

"Still sounds like a viable candidate," Hennessy says as he opens the Snapple. "You said there's an eyewitness."

"Yeah," Fendrick grimaces. "A guy lives with his sister when he's not up in the mountains. In his forties, says he's a retired software engineer. Running gear and a Willie Nelson T-shirt. He ID'd Broner, said he saw the shooting and the robbery. We picked Broner up right away. He was in the area, but no watch, no wallet, no briefcase, no gun."

"What do you think?"

"Mann could've seen him anywhere, might be mistaken."

"Did you get a GSR swab?"

"The state trooper that picked him up swabbed him right away. The guy's hands smelled of gasoline, so he might have wiped them down, and he's already claiming he was here helping a friend replace brake pads, and decided to go sightseeing. So it doesn't look good."

"You've lost me," says Hennessy. Callahan looks up from his notes.

"Gunshot residue from the primer can show that someone has fired a gun. Unfortunately it can be washed off and similar particles can come from other sources, such as car brake pads." Hennessey nods his understanding.

"You've searched the area?" Greene asks. Fendrick makes an unhappy face.

"Nothing."

"So, he had an accomplice?" Greene offers.

"Maybe, but here's the real problem. A robbery gone bad is all that works here. The witness claims, and we've pushed him, that Broner called out Dixon's name, and when they were face to face, shot him. Then he robbed him." Hennessy looks confused again.

"It doesn't add up," explains Callahan. "It's early, but we can't find any connection between Dixon and Broner. If it's a random robbery, Broner wouldn't know Dixon's name. A robbery gone bad, there would have been resistance before the shooting. The witness says Broner shot Dixon, then robbed him."

"Anything else on the witness?" asks Greene.

"Not yet. There's a prior address out in southern California. We'll call in a couple hours when they wake up out there, talk to the local cops, cover the bases."

"What about the sister?"

"Younger than her brother. Seems legit, some kind of freelance photographer," says Fendrick. "Sort of a freelance family."

"What's next," Greene looks at the two cops.

"We're going to talk to Jonny Carson." Greene's eyebrows go up.

"Thought he was dead. I miss him."

"No, really," Callahan says. "Broner's pal with the brake pads. See if he backs up the story Broner gave us."

"Could it still be a hit?" asks Greene. Fendrick shakes his head.

"The witness is confused," Fendrick wrinkles his nose. "He'll think about it and change his story." He looks at Callahan and back to Greene. "The guy strikes me as flaky, that there's something wrong. The victim, Kenneth Dixon, was a forensic accountant with the title of Senior Investigator with the State Department of Agriculture. In his forties, been there a while. We'll talk to his supervisors, see what he was working on, but still, who whacks the farm guy?"

Greene frowns and stares out the window. "I know of Dixon. He's made some high profile collars in his time with Ag. Mostly money laundering, that kind of stuff." Greene looks at the ADA. "When is the arraignment, Joe?"

"Late morning. We should be able to keep him without bail. Once he gets counsel, though, it'll get harder. Specially if the witness is all we've got and there's questions."

"Keep me in the loop," Greene says as he stands. "Nothing to indicate Dixon was a target. The witness is the only link that Broner had anything to do with it. Keep looking. If anything changes let me know. Meantime I'll give the US Attorney's Office a heads up." Greene looks at the young assistant DA. "Joe, are you aware of anything in the US Code that would disqualify a witness because he's a Willie Nelson fan?" Greene smiles at Hennessy's confused look, turns and walks out the door.

4

Police Court, Albany, New York

"Watch out, asshole," Jason Broner stumbles over a man dressed like an exotic bird. The narrow hall between the cells quickly fills with the haul from the prior day and night, prisoners not yet sporting the standard orange jumpsuit. Sunlight barely passes through the high barred windows into the disorderly crowd. Neon lights spark and sputter overhead, deputies with clubs keep order.

"Fuck you, shithead," the bird replies. A truncheon appears between them.

"Cause me any trouble and I'll put you back in the pit. It's nowhere near the forty eight the law calls for," the deputy with the dead eyes is all business. Broner and the bird glare at each other, shut up, and waddle, leg irons clanking, to their places to await the next act.

"Hey honey pie." A loud suit approaches the bird. "What you gone and done this time?"

"Just more of the same, Roger. These cops just don't like us trannys, and you know it."

"Don't you worry, honey, bail and fine, ain't gonna be no time."

Broner is watching the door opposite, the one the guy in the cheap suit came through. Would there be someone coming in to represent him? Maybe Jonny would get somebody, but then Jonny had no real money, and no contacts. He thinks that if he can get a half decent public defender maybe he can get the charges dropped. Broner isn't real sure why they picked him up, what they know. What could they have on him?

Several more legal types come in and meet up with their clients. Then it's time for the court appointeds to come in and meet theirs.

"Hi there, are you Jordan Broner?"

"Jason Broner."

"Oh yeah, sorry. I spilled some coffee, blotted out your first name. I'm Clarence Chase. I'll be entering your plea, working on your case."

Broner looks at the boyish face, the pudginess in a rumpled suit, and his eyes darken. The door opens and the deputy motions them to follow him into the courtroom.

"Sit here till your case is called. No messing around. The judge won't like it," the deputy then leans against the door with his arms folded. Chase looks at the papers in his hand as he talks to his client.

"We'll enter the plea and meet later," Chase looks at Broner hopefully. "I have a few people still to see this morning." Broner just stares at him, unblinking. "We'll catch up at the County jail, and talk about your case. How to proceed."

The strike of the gavel brings silence to the room. The dance commences, the actors speak their practiced lines and play their rehearsed roles. Public defenders stand on cue, listen to the charges, declare their clients innocence, and make note of details for the next act.

"Lets go, time to move on." The bored deputy keeps the morning flow of justice on track. Chase seems fine with that and bumps and jostles his way nervously from the courtroom. A sullen Jason Broner is led back to the holding cell.

5

North Albany

Fendrick drives as Callahan checks out numbers on the dilapidated structures in the rundown industrial park in Albany's north end. The odd mixture of block buildings, ramshackle wooden structures, the odd Quonset hut, and vacant lots with old tires and bottles peeking through the weeds speak to an economy in free fall.

"There it is," announces Callahan pointing at a garage. "If Broner's right that's Jonny Carson's place."

The blue Chevy pulls into the yard, finds a place among the scattered cars, all in various stages of decline. A ten-foot chain link fence seems to define the property's side boundaries, while the vintage Quonset hut takes up most of the space in between. A narrow track runs down the side of the building to the deep lot behind, where there's a hint of more vehicle cadavers. The front of a cherry red Mustang can be seen inside the shadow of the hut.

"Nice place," says Fendrick as he opens the door and levers himself out from behind the wheel. Callahan joins him and they approach the partially open garage door.

"Help you?" The voice comes from the outside corner of the building, near the fence. A short thin man is busily pouring gasoline over his hands and drying them with a dirty rag. An oil barrel is set up next to him, like a workbench. On it are what could only be brake components.

***

Half an hour later they drive away from Jonny Carson's place of business.

"OK, Carson backs up Broner's story, so he has an excuse for the gas on his hands, whenever it got there. And the brake pad thing could

17

be used to compromise the GSR if any shows up. So we got nothing here." Fendrick is thinking out loud, frustrated.

"Yeah, but we've still got the witness."

"Yeah, but our witness doesn't seem to have the order right, the way things happened. That'll be a problem if this worm ever dumps Chase and gets himself a real lawyer." Fendrick shakes his head. "This should be a clean solve for us and a win for the DA. We better get Mann back in and straighten him out."

"Don't forget we need to check out his background. Call out west, talk to the local cops, have they ever heard of him. His old employer, see if the 'patent' story checks out. If Broner does get a real lawyer this could be tough, we don't need any surprises."

"Maybe we should talk to the sister, try to get a read. There's something about this guy that makes me nervous, ever since I asked him to get in the car yesterday."

"You gonna give Agent Greene an update on his friend, Jonny Carson?"

"Fuck Greene."

6

Albany County Jail

Broner sits nervously, he's been waiting for a while now. The room is prison dull with no air circulating. He starts as the door opens and Clarence Chase, Esq. is shown in by the guard. Chase looks like a guy who likes to go along and get along. Broner looks like a guy who doesn't like him.

"Good morning, Jason. Sorry I'm late. Court." He smiles.

Broner stares at him.

"Where do I stand?"

"OK. Well, I spoke to the ADA. He's met with the detectives and they'll prepare a case. In your favor, there was no evidence found on you, or anywhere around the crime scene. You have an alibi for being in the area, helping your friend Jonny with his car. There is no indication that you knew the victim, or had any reason to wish him harm. They'll have a hard time with motive. If the GSR comes back negative or unclear there's no physical evidence."

"What's not in my 'favor'?"

"Well, the real problem is that they have an eyewitness. The man claims he saw the shooting, and he has identified you as the shooter."

Broner's eyes narrow as he digests this. A witness.

"Will that stand up?"

"Well, that's hard to say. We don't know much about him yet, but we're looking into it. Eyewitness accounts aren't given the weight today that they once had. Too many times found to be unreliable, and very often the basis for appeal. If we can discredit the witness in some way, I don't think they have a case. Keep in mind, though, Dixon was in State law enforcement. They may not let this go without a fight, and according to the assistant district attorney I talked to, worst case, it could even go Federal."

"What's that mean?"

Chase takes a deep breath.

"There seems to be some question as to the sequence of events."

"What's that mean?" Broner is now getting agitated, and louder. Chase glances at the door.

"The cops think the witness is confused, which could help us," Chase says. Broner stares at him. "The cops want to solve this as a robbery gone bad. If the witness is to be believed, the sequence would indicate that the objective was to murder Mr. Dixon and make it look like a robbery attempt."

"What's the difference?" barks Broner.

"If they believe the witness and decide it was a murder from the start, the FBI takes over." Chase licks his lips, a light sheen of sweat appears on his forehead. "Everything gets kicked up a notch."

"What's a notch?"

Chase looks at his hands.

"I must advise that the premeditated killing of a state law enforcement official is a very serious crime, and the prosecutor could ask for the death penalty. Historically the feds aren't likely to look for that unless it involves an act of terrorism, but it still gets very serious, and a guilty verdict would mean a Federal facility for life, without parole."

Broner doesn't respond, other than to purse his lips as his eyes narrow.

7

Montreal, Canada

Jurga is talking to her second cousin in California. Jurga is desperate, her cousin has to help. Outside her window the sprinkler sweeps back and forth, green grass sparkling in the afternoon Canadian sunshine.

"Mika, they started arriving by post two weeks ago." She's talking about the photos of her parents back in Ukraine. Not vacation snaps. "They are out working in the garden and don't know that someone is photographing them. There is a bulls eye drawn around each of their faces."

Mika, older than Jurga by ten years, a Californian for fifteen, is not easily disturbed.

"Jurga, maybe it's just a sick joke. You know that some have held it against you and Robert, getting an education and moving to Canada, the jobs you have, and now the twins. They hate you for your success." They? Jurga thought, then quickly dismissed it. This is about her children's safety.

"Maybe these photos, but not the ones Robert got, they are no joke."

"Robert got photos, too?"

"His widowed mother in her sitting room, staring at the camera. There are three men standing behind her wearing masks. They have their penises in their hands. It's clear what they intend."

"Oh my God!"

"You have to help me. You have to take the twins until this is over."

"What do you mean by 'over'?"

"You know how they work. They're going to make us do something, we don't know what yet. They're showing us what will happen if we don't do as they say. We think they'll let us know soon what it is." Deep breath. "We think we'll have to do it, whatever it is. I don't want my children around this. I don't want to be around this."

8

Townhouse in Albany

"More coffee? Another bagel?"

"Are you trying to fatten me up?"

"Look, you run too much and eat too little. You're six feet and barely a hundred seventy pounds. You probably don't eat at all when you go up north." I can't help but smile at the concern on my sister's face.

"It helps keep me sane, I think." Oops. Shouldn't have gone there.

She sits down across from me, her blue eyes suddenly sad. The kitchen is cozy and full of sunlight, but the mood has changed quickly. She takes my hand in both of hers and holds tightly. I think about how much she's helped me, and realize how easily I forget that she's been through a lot as well. And that someone she still loves has died, too. I squeeze back and offer a weak smile. I feel some of the warmth return.

"I'll make it till lunch without needing intravenous. After that, I don't know."

"You can joke all you want, but I know you forget to eat sometimes, like the other night when you got home from the police station, all you'd had was their cup of coffee."

"Just to keep the record straight, I did not drink their coffee. It was awful."

Yvette is five years younger then me, trim and athletic, her long black hair and blue eyes in contrast to my light brown hair and green eyes. She smiles as she takes the dishes to the sink and rinses them. I pick up the paper again and reread the obituary.

"He was quite a guy. Veteran, law school grad, accounting degree. Left a wife, two married sons. Family originally from up north."

She turns from the sink and looks at me, hands knotting the dishcloth.

"After everything, are you sure you should go to the funeral?"

I study my hands for a moment before answering, then look up at those deep pools of blue, those eyes that always look for me.

"I sort of feel I owe it to him. I saw him die. It might give me some closure, too. I have no real role here, none of it is about me. I can hang in the wings, be invisible. Learn to cope on my own." I smile up at my sister. "Want to come along?"

Her smile lights up the room, but she still shakes her head no.

"I can't. I have a meeting today with that National Geographic rep about a possible shoot in France."

"When would it be?"

"Not sure exactly, but it will be after the trip to Ireland." She drops the dishcloth on the counter and turns to me. "Oh shit! Are you still able to go with me, what with the trial and all?"

"I'll give them a call later today, after the funeral."

She puts a light jacket on over her blouse and ties her hair into a ponytail. The bag with her laptop goes over her shoulder. I get a kiss on the cheek and she's out the door.

I go to dig out my dark suit, trying not to think about the last time I wore it.

9

Homicide Division

Fendrick flops down in his chair and lets out a long sigh. Callahan looks at him and stifles a yawn.

"How was court?"

Fendrick snorts.

"Same old shit. Sat on my ass trying to look serious for an hour and then they adjourned over some dumb fuck-up by the prosecution. They'll let me know when to come back. Like I got nothing else to do." Fendrick snorts again. "Did you get a chance to follow up out west with Mann?" There's an edge to Fendrick's voice.

"Got to his last employer. Human Resources. Gave me dates, said everything was satisfactory, left of his own accord to pursue other opportunities. Did seem a little hesitant, maybe overly careful. West Coast, you never know. Didn't get a chance to call any law enforcement."

"I got some time now. Give me that address and I'll try to figure out the closest jurisdiction." Callahan holds up his legal pad, points at an address and tosses it over. Fendrick turns to his computer and starts calling up search engines. He begins with Mann's name and California address.

Callahan jumps as Fendrick's back straightens and his fist slams the desk.

"I knew it!"

* * *

"Hold on, please, Detective Fendrick. I'll connect you to Chief O'Donnell's office now." Callahan can see Fendrick's jaw muscles still working as he cradles the phone, pad and pen ready to go.

"Chief O'Donnell's office, how can I help you?"

"Hello. This is Detective Fendrick with the Albany, New York, Police Department. I'd like to speak with the Chief, please."

"I'm sorry, Detective Fendrick, but the Chief is out at a crime scene right now. What does this concern, maybe someone else can help you."

"We have a witness to a murder who used to live in your area, and I need to check him out. I've seen some disturbing headlines on the Internet about him, but the stories are gone, all it says is the content has been removed."

"What's the witness's name, sir?"

"John Mann."

Fendrick waits, knows the person has their hand over the phone and is talking to someone else, then they come back.

"I'm sorry, Detective Fendrick, but you will have to talk to the Chief about that. Please give me your details. I'm sure he'll call as soon as he returns."

Fendrick gets off the phone and looks at Callahan, palms raised, mouth open wide in disbelief, a tic noticeable over his left eye..

"What's going on here? I didn't like this guy from the start, but he murdered his wife and daughter? Great witness we got."

"There must be more to it. Are you sure that's everything the search engine found? No article at all, just those blurbs?"

"I'm sure, alright. Can't wait to hear back from this chief." He's beating the pen on the desk, his fist white knuckled, face purple. Callahan looks at the clock.

"We better get a move on if we're going to make that funeral."

10

Downtown Albany

The Hilton Hotel is a short walk from the townhouse in Center Square. Yvette walks it in ten minutes. The meeting room on the first floor is just off the lobby, with long windows overlooking the city center and views of the Hudson River. The door is open and she can see the well dressed and coiffed woman she once knew. Yvette knocks and walks in.

"Yvette! So good to see you again."

"Hi, Jodi. Good to see you."

"Wow, you still look like you could walk on center court and play six sets. How'd you keep that figure?" Jodi turns to a younger woman who appears to be an assistant of some sort and introduces her as Emma. "I haven't seen this girl since senior year in high school," she gushes, holding Yvette at arms length, getting a good look. "Yvette was a star tennis player all through school, colleges on the east coast were drooling for her to take their scholarships."

"I'm just a poor photographer these days Jodi, chasing some work." Jodi cocks her head to one side, beaming.

"Did you ever marry that hunk from the football team? Is that why you gave up the scholarships?"

"No. That didn't work out. I went to Berkley instead. That's where I got into the film work." It's awkward, all right. Three of them stand around with dopey smiles. Yvette considers giving them the Cliff's Notes version of her life since High School, leaving them open mouthed as she turns, head high, and storms out. Instead she goes with, "So, tell me about this job in France. Sounds real interesting." Jodi's smile fades a little, returns to the task at hand.

"Have a seat, sweetie. I think you're going to like this. How do you feel about prehistoric cave art?"

11

Emmanual Baptist Church, Albany, NY

I drive past the church and see that a large crowd has already gathered. I have to park a couple of blocks away. As I walk up the street I see Fendrick and Callahan pull up to a No Parking area in front of the church and display their POLICE creds. They hurry in a side door. Probably a 'No Entry' point. They don't see me, and I feel OK with that. I join a crowd that goes in through the front door.

While people slowly move forward looking for seats I move sideways and find a place to stand against the back wall. I have a good vantage point, and can see that Kenneth Dixon had been well thought of. There are a lot of uniforms, a lot of suits, and a lot of black veils. I can see the backs of the figures in the crowded front pew and figure the widow and her sons and their families are there. A casket sits in the center aisle in front of the altar. There are candles on it, and I can smell incense. Looking at it I feel a chill. I focus on forcing old, but still fresh, memories from my mind. I realize my clasped hands are shaking.

The minister starts with some prayers, a service I'm not familiar with, but that shows great dignity and reverence. There are readings by family members. Then the minister steps down from the altar and stands next to the coffin. He places his hand on the dark wood in a familiar way, a way that says he knew Kenneth Dixon well.

"When I first met Kenneth I asked him a question I ask each member of our congregation. What informs your Christianity? Why do you believe?" The minister looks at the casket with a soft chuckle. He shares a knowing look with the widow.

"Julia, would you like to tell this story?"

The small noises you hear in every church stop. No coughs, no rustling of clothing, no whispers. An attractive woman rises in the front pew and makes her way to the side of the coffin. She, too, puts her hand on the shining surface with such a loving touch. She takes a deep breath and faces the congregation.

"My husbands family had what became to them a famous interaction with an Irish family back in 1834 in Big Moose, in the Adirondack Mountains, up north of here. Ken always said it all began in Big Moose. I guess he meant in part his struggle, and his family's, to bridge the chasm of being black in a white world."

She pauses and looks at the coffin.

"Well, there was an immigrant family on their way to Ohio where they had relations. They'd sailed from Cobh in Ireland to Canada on what people now call coffin ships. They were the Shaws. They survived the voyage and got as far as Big Moose, but by then the children had typhoid, the mother was sick from the cold, they had no money, and no friends. The people that lived around there at the time would have nothing to do with them because they were Irish. Imagine that!"

I hear some soft laughter.

"It was November, and the winter was just getting underway. My husband's family had suffered some by that time because of their color, but they worked hard on their small farm, and had put up as much in stores and cut firewood as they could. Like everyone at that time, though, they knew it would be barely enough to get through. But they did not even consider turning that family away."

Julia Dixon lifts her chin, even as she looks at her husband's coffin, showing pride for what he stood for.

"They took that family in and nursed the children and the mother to health, fed them and kept them warm until the spring. The father did what he could to help. When the spring thaw came the Shaw's continued their trip to Ohio, and the Dixon's, my husband's people, took as creed that race didn't matter. Helping each other was what counted. For generations it was that experience that was used in the family history to underscore that people needed to help each other, and that race had nothing to do with it. It was a creed that Ken grew up with, and that informed everything he did in life. That's why Ken used to say, 'It all began in Big Moose'."

She smiles and goes back to her seat. The minister looks out over the assembly.

"And that's the Ken Dixon we all knew."

There are more prayers, a good few songs, beautifully done, and then the casket is taken out, followed by the family. I work my way into the line leaving the church, but it's slow going. When I clear the door I see why. Julia Dixon and her sons are shaking hands and thanking each person as they leave.

Fendrick and Callahan are about ten people ahead of me. Fendrick looks back and spots me. His face turns red and his eyes bug out. He starts towards me, but Callahan grabs him and holds him back. As I get closer to the reception line I hear Fendrick talking to Julia Dixon, who turns to stare at me. I can only make out bits of what he says. "….watched your husband get….and did nothing…might have…killed…wife and daughter…"

I didn't meet Julia Dixon. I barely recall going back into the church and out a side door, sneaking back to my car like a guilty man, fighting nausea and tunnel vision. But I am not guilty here. Of anything. I've learned to deal with the old guilt, finally. There will be no new guilt. There's nothing to be afraid of. I tell myself that I am safe.

12

Townhouse in Albany

I sit at the kitchen table. The front door opens, and Yvette comes in and throws her bag on the table. She gets herself a glass of water and sits across from me. She doesn't look happy.

"How'd it go? Did you get the job?" She makes a funny face as she looks at me.

"I did get it. It sounds really interesting. The timing is right, too. I can go to France right from Ireland. The team is strong, and I've worked with a couple of them before."

"Well, sounds good. But something didn't go well, right?" She deflates and starts moving her water glass, making wet circles on the red formica.

"The woman doing the interview. I knew her in school in California. She's married with kids, overweight, settled into her life, real comfortable."

"Not someone I'd expect you to envy, or be bothered by."

"No. That's not it. She remembered I was a tennis ace with scholarships back east. She remembered the jock with the scouts crawling all over him, and that we were together."

"Oh. She started to ask questions?"

"I almost walked out. What was I supposed to do? Tell her he knocked me up and our parents forced me to have a back street abortion so 'we' wouldn't ruin our lives? Tell her it went wrong and I can't have kids now? Tell her I regret that abortion more than anything in my life? Tell her he dropped me then, that I rebelled and said fuck tennis, and ran off to be a hippy at Berkley?"

Yvette's eyes fill up with tears. I stand and go to her, wrap my arms around her shoulders and feel her sobs. In just a few moments it's over.

She composes herself, as always. She pats my arms and hugs them. I kiss the top of her head. I sit back down. Yvette dries her eyes and gives me a weak smile.

"So, how was the funeral?"

"It was beautiful. Dixon was well thought of, the minister apparently knew him well, asked his widow to tell a family story. Lots of songs, some readings. Nice."

"Did you meet Mrs. Dixon?" I really don't want to tell her this part, but I'm stuck. I don't want to lie to her, and besides, I'll never get away with it, she knows me too well. So I tell her about the receiving line, Fendrick and Callahan, and what I'd overheard.

My sister goes ballistic.

And heads for the phone.

13

Montreal, Canada

Jurga sits at the dining room table, the cup of tea in front of her untouched. The upscale home is on a tributary of the St. Lawrence River outside of Montreal, and reflects her and her husband's status as professionals. She hears the car pull into the driveway and park in front of the garage. A car door slams. As the side door leading into the kitchen opens she hears Robert's cheerful voice.

"Jurga, darling, I'm home."

He walks into the dining room and stops. His eyes go from Jurga to the envelope on the table and his face sinks into despair. He sits down next to her and puts his arm around her.

"Please let it be instructions, what they will make us do," she sobs. "I fear it, but we can't live like this. Waiting, not knowing, pretending we're not under the knife." Robert pulls her closer to him and caresses her face.

After a moment he says, "Let's see what it is."

His fingers shake as he carefully works the flap open. One page with explicit instructions drops out. There is a container in their garage. They will deliver it on Sunday.

"Oh my God!" Jurga is shaking as she rocks back and forth, holding her knees. "They've been here!"

14

Albany County

Fendrick and Callahan drive north to Watervliet, a smaller city in the same county. They park behind the long, low building off the beaten path and enter the cool darkness through a side door. The room holds about ten tables, most empty after the noontime rush. Double doors lead off the far side into the bar, where a television is on low, the occasional knock as a glass hits the wooden bar. They take a formica topped table in a far corner and settle into the bentwood chairs as the waitress approaches.

"What'll it be today, boys?"

"Cheeseburger with fries, and the coldest bottle of Bud you got," Fendrick orders.

"I'll have the fish n' chips and a diet coke," Callahan says.

The waitress leaves and Callahan turns to his partner.

"Calm down, Fendrick, you're letting this get to you. You know you shouldn't have said anything to the widow about Mann. We still don't know what's going on there."

"You can fuck off, too. This idiot Mann is going to ruin this case. I'm not even sure we've got the right guy based on Mann as a witness. Every time I turn around the guy gets flakier."

"Maybe it wasn't a robbery. Did you ever think of that?"

"Not you, too. Next you'll be sucking up to that feebee, Greene."

"I'm just saying, until we talk to that Chief out in California we don't know what the story on Mann is."

"Whatever it is, it won't be good. Everything about this case stinks."

Callahan lets out a sigh. He grabs a newspaper from a nearby table and starts to read the sports page.

"I'll have another beer, honey."

Callahan glances up, sees Fendricks' glare, and goes back to his paper.

It's another hour and two more beers before they get back to the station and get the message that the Chief from California had returned their call.

"He say anything else?" Fendrick is surlier than usual to the sergeant.

"He said he'd call back at four, our time," she replies.

"OK." Fendrick starts to turn towards his office.

"One more thing." Fendrick turns back to the sergeant.

"Yeah?"

"He sounded really pissed off."

15

Homicide Division

Three of them sit around the table as four o'clock approaches. Callahan insisted that Hennessy join them so that the attorney can evaluate what Chief O'Donnell has to tell them, and how it could affect the credibility of their witness and the case against Broner. The conference phone rings and Callahan hits the button as Fendrick leans forward.

"Hello, Chief. This is Detective Fendrick with the Albany Police Department. We're on a conference line. With me is Detective Callahan and assistant district attorney Hennessy. Thanks for getting back to us."

"I nearly went right to your Chief, and I might still. Yvette Mann tells me you're going around accusing her brother of murdering his wife and child. Is that right?"

Hennessy's eyes go wide as saucers. Callahan's shoulders sag as he looks over at Fendrick, who does a double take.

"Well, er, that's what we're calling about. We saw some Internet headlines, but the content was removed."

"Do you guys go through any training before they hand you a badge? Did it ever occur to you to have this talk before making accusations?"

Fendrick is a little pale, then a little splotchy.

"Chief, that was a mistake," Callahan says, "no doubt about it. Can you tell us what's going on here? Mann is a witness to a robbery that turned into a murder, and we're trying to sort out how dependable a witness we've got."

They hear a loud exhale on the other end of the line.

"Eight years ago John Mann went to his lawyer to sign documents suing for the divorce of his wife and custody of his daughter. When he got back his house had burned to the ground, and the fire marshals had located the two bodies, his wife and daughter. Mann fell to his knees on his front lawn, hysterical, screaming that he had killed them, that he was guilty. I wasn't Chief then, I was still with CHiPS, but got involved as support later. This wasn't a professional department then, much like it seems you have in Albany."

The Chief pauses.

"The cops on the scene cuffed Mann, read him his rights, and put him in the back of a squad car. He spent the night in jail. The poor bastard nearly went crazy. By the next morning the headlines in the paper, which apparently you found, said 'Mann Guilty in Death of Wife and Daughter', and 'Husband Admits He Did It'."

"Are you saying he didn't do it?" says Fendrick.

"Who woke you up? No he didn't do it. Once the Highway Patrol got involved and a proper investigation was done it was clear that the wife, an alcoholic, fell asleep on the sofa while smoking. While on fire she apparently ran to the crib to try to save the child, spreading the fire. They both burned to death. Didn't die of smoke inhalation. Burned to death."

There's silence as the impact of these words settle in.

"So why did Mann say he was guilty?"

There's a longer pause before the Chief responds.

"Maybe I will call your Chief. I can recommend some training modules that cover subjects like human nature, the psychology of grief and loss, you know, stuff cops are supposed to know about when they look for motive. Mann took it hard. Why didn't I act sooner? Why did I leave my daughter with her? Why didn't I get her help? Why did I desert my family and go to a lawyer? Take your pick. Mann took it personally, took responsibility for the loss of his family. And got treated like a murderer."

"That's terrible Chief. What happened to him?" Callahan asks. Another long sigh.

"Well, I'm Chief now. We got Mann all the help we could, the city paid for it. Our insurers dropped us, and our corporation counsel got ready for a lawsuit that would bankrupt us."

"Did he sue you?" Hennessy finally finds something in the exchange that he can speak to.

"That's the funny thing. No, he didn't. And as soon as he recovered enough to be back on his own he paid for his treatment. He even signed a hold harmless agreement that said he wouldn't sue us, and that allowed the city to get coverage and not have to create a self-insurance fund. We convinced the newspapers to get rid of their content on threat of becoming co-defendants in the destruction of the man. There was a proviso, of course, that involved no further disruption of his life as a result of this matter. Which of course is why his sister just carved me a new asshole."

"We're really sorry about that Chief. We'll make it right on our end."

"Your Callahan, right?"

"Yes, sir."

"So, Fendrick, you're the lunkhead that did this. I might just call your Chief and corporation counsel; see what they think of the potential liability you've created. The thought of you walking your beat emptying parking meters would make me feel a lot better." He pauses again, then a resigned sigh. "The truth is, Mann won't sue you. He's just not like that, and the last thing he wants is notoriety. He's still healing. His sister, though? She'd take the whole lot of you out and drown you. Are we done here?"

The two detectives and the lawyer are still sitting staring at the dead phone when the sergeant knocks and comes in.

"Capitol Police are here. They have a video of Dixon's murder they say you have to see."

16

Albany, New York

This time they meet in the James T. Foley U.S. Courthouse, an Art Deco treasure from the 1930's located on Broadway in downtown Albany. They are hosted by James Ostermann, one of the United States attorneys representing the US District Court for the Northern District of New York.

"Coffee?" asks Ostermann's PA.

"Black, one sugar," says Greene.

Hennessy pulls a Snapple from his briefcase. Greene raises up a little to see inside the leather satchel, expecting to see an apple or a banana. Callahan refuses a beverage. Fendrick hasn't shown up this morning, so Callahan and Hennessy came without him.

Hennessy clears his throat.

"These are copies of our files, everything should be in there. A copy of the Capitol Police tape is there, too."

"We'll go over it carefully," Ostermann begins. "This is the evidence that convinced you this was not a messed up robbery?"

"Yes," says Hennessy. "Although we can't positively ID Broner, it does appear to be him, and every action that the man takes is exactly as described by the witness, who identified Broner as the man on the tape."

"So we've got a murder on our hands," Greene says. "From the looks of it, a murder for hire."

"It would seem so," agrees Callahan.

"Looks likely we can get a conviction on Broner, he can do life," adds Ostermann. "Unless he wants to give up whoever hired him."

"That's the big question," says Greene. "The witness and the tape are going to make this case airtight. You had misgivings about this witness earlier. What happened?" Hennessy, to his credit, takes this one.

"He'd had a tragic event in his past. It involved the death of his wife and daughter. At that time he was wrongly accused and arrested. The detectives picked up that something was wrong, but it never came out until they investigated further. They initially thought that he jumbled the sequence of events. Happens all the time with witnesses." Greene notices Callahan's look of surprise at Hennessy's adept explanation. Ostermann is finished with them.

"Agent Greene and I will review the files, talk to Broner's attorney about the change in prosecution, and let you know if we need you to follow up on anything. Fair enough?"

They rise to leave, turn towards the door. Hennessy stops and turns back, holds up a hand.

"Oh, before I forget," he says. "Mann called yesterday and asked about a trip to Ireland he'd planned with his sister, its next week. She has some work there. A few days. I asked Fendrick, he said no way. I haven't called Mann back yet."

Greene and Ostermann exchange a look, then a nod.

"I think, all things considered, we can tell Mr. Mann that'll be fine," Greene says.

As the two men walk out the front doors of the federal building Callahan angrily pulls at his tie to loosen it.

"Asshole," he spits.

Hennessy looks for a moment like he's going to ask a question, then thinks better of it.

17

Albany County Jail

Jason Broner has been looking forward to his lunch, if only because it breaks the monotony of time spent in the County jail. As he watches the trusty work his way down the rows of cells he sees the jailer coming through. He stops in front of Broner.

"Your attorney wants to see you." Broner's expression says he wonders what the dipshit wants. At the same time he's hopeful that the witness has cracked, that he'll be getting out. Chase has told him the cop, Fendrick, doesn't like the guy, thinks he's flakey. There's no evidence, just that witness. Maybe.

Those hopes fade when he sees Chase' face.

Chase settles in with his closed briefcase placed between them on the table, a barrier, protection.

"I got a call from the US Attorney," Chase absently pats the lapel of his brown suit. "They found a CCTV of the shooting. They can't ID you definitively from the tape, but it looks like you, and they can easily see what transpired. It follows the witness' account in every detail."

"You told me the cops thought he got it wrong, was confused."

"The credibility that the tape gives his story also gives credibility to his identification of you." Broner hunches forward, fixing his hooded eyes on Chase.

"What does that mean?" Broner's question leaves Chase momentarily frustrated.

"They've pretty much got you. The case has gone federal. About all we can do is try to get the charges knocked down, see if we can get less than life with no parole."

Broner takes a deep breath and sits back. His dark eyes narrow, the thick brows almost touch. He stares at his hands. When he looks back up at Chase his jaw sets.

"OK, let's say I took a contract." He becomes more intense. Chase places his hands against his briefcase, shoring up the barrier. Broner goes on. "Let's say I know the people. Let's say these people are big. Big money, big network, big names. Think *mafiya*. Let's say I have info on them that they don't know about." Chase swallows hard but says nothing. "I need a deal. Soon. I need witness protection. These people find out I know who they are they'll kill me. I can't hide from them. They'll get me inside, first day."

Chase clears his throat. "I can call the US Attorney. Meet with him. See if they have any interest in some kind of deal."

Broner puts his head in his hands, then raises his eyes and looks at Chase.

"Problem is, you don't have the balls for this. I need someone who's been around. Somebody that's not going to be scared shitless of these people, like you are."

Chase sits up straight in his chair, teasing a look of indignation across his features, an effort that is soon belied by his words.

"Jason, these are serious charges that could result in a life sentence. You need to have confidence in your defense team. If for some reason you don't feel comfortable with me, we can petition for a change of counsel."

Broner closes his eyes for a second and then looks at Chase again.

"How do I know I won't wind up with another shit bird like you?"

Chase's face lights up like an inspiration has struck, forgets to pretend to be insulted. "I went to law school with a guy. His father's a famous attorney, takes on this kind of work. Some family stuff, goes back a long way. Doesn't like the people you mentioned. If it's the right people, he works pro bono."

"Bono?" Broner looks confused.

"Free, he works for free if he gets to go after some of these Russians. I can see if he'll talk to you?" The look Broner gives him makes Chase feel faint.

"Do it," Broner says.

18

Townhouse in Albany

Greene says goodbye and I hang up the phone. Yvette comes into the kitchen. She's been in the spare room working out on the kickboxing bag. She raises her eyebrows.

"Well?"

"That was Agent Greene," I say as she hands me a cup of coffee and sits down. "No more Fendrick or Callahan. Seems I belong to him now."

"How nice. Do I get to visit the two of you?"

"Well, me, anyway. They believe me now. Not a robbery gone wrong anymore. Murder of a state law enforcement officer."

"How come the promotion?"

"Seems the Capitol Police came up with some CCTV that shows the killing, and that it happened the way I said. That convinced them that it was actually intended to be a murder and not a robbery."

"So why Greene?"

"Dixon was state law enforcement. Federal crime."

"Is this good?" she says.

"It's probably good. At least Greene doesn't seem to hate me. This part you'll like, he said its OK to take that trip to Ireland we planned. Only bad thing is he doesn't think I'll be able to go to France on the National Geographic shoot with you. Could be trial time." Yvette clasps her hands and jumps up and down in her chair.

"But we can go to Ireland? That's great! I'll give Janice a call and tell her the reservations are good, and we'll be using them."

19

Empire State Plaza, Albany

"Hello, Agent Greene. What can I do for you?"

Elias Bezaan gazes through the floor to ceiling windows of his office overlooking the Empire State Plaza. From where he sits he can just see the famous 'Egg', an architectural wonder resulting from a continuous concrete pour. After three decades of making the right moves in the Machiavellian state bureaucracy Elias Bezaan finally has the corner office.

"Thanks for taking my call, Mr. Bezaan. I know how busy you must be."

"No problem. I understand this has to do with our Investigator, Kenneth Dixon." 'Our', not 'my', Greene notes.

"I'm not sure if anyone has updated you on the investigation, but right now we feel certain that Mr. Dixon was murdered. The robbery was just an attempt to cover that up."

"Such a shame, in any event."

"Yes. It also raises the question of why Mr. Dixon was murdered. The suspect that has been identified as the killer would have no reason that we can find other than if he was hired to do it. We're looking into why someone would want to have Mr. Dixon killed, and I'm wondering if it could be something related to his job. Something he was working on?"

"Hmm…" Bezaan admires his view for a few seconds before answering. "I don't know of anything that would give rise to that kind of reaction. Most of our work here is fairly mundane. True, our investigators do keep their activities pretty much to themselves until something is actionable, then our legal people get involved. I can check with some of his co-workers, see if they're aware of anything. Nothing has come to my attention, however."

"Dixon did initiate some fairly high profile prosecutions, involving money laundering, right?"

"My agency is always on the lookout for that. For some reason the industry – agriculture, fertilizer, food prep, production and sales – seems to lend itself to those activities."

"But nothing you know of recently?"

"No, but I will make inquiries, as I said. If anything comes up I'll contact you."

"OK, Mr. Bezaan. We'll leave at it that for the time being. Just so you understand, though, we're the FBI. I work with Federal Prosecutors. We have subpoena power. We put people under oath. Unfortunately, sometimes that results in their own inadequacies and mistakes coming out. I expect to hear back from you, Mr. Bezaan. I expect some answers. I'm investigating a murder, not a land dispute. Am I clear?"

"Of course, Agent Greene. I'm sure we'll talk soon."

Bezaan replaces the handset and stares at the phone for a few moments. Reluctantly he picks up the receiver and dials a Manhattan number.

20

Manhattan, New York

Boris waits until everyone has their drink, conversations muted by the plush carpet and rich furnishings of the boardroom, the one percent of the one percent make their way to their usual seats.

"How could a black man possibly understand how a free society must be structured in order to function?" enquires the son of a steel magnate.

"It's this whole voting thing that's to blame. We have to once again get control. We should have learned that lesson when Gore almost broke through. Since then it's been abysmal." This from a coal industry scion.

Boris watches and listens as the comfortable conversations, begun at the elegant mahogany and brass bar in the adjacent room, wind down. The people sitting around the table have the look of money. Old money. The highly polished dark oak, the smell of leather, subdued lighting, mahogany walls, and expensive art didn't hurt that impression.

They look up expectantly as Boris stands. He's at one end of the table, with the eldest, richest, most venerable of this group at the other. The rest fill the ranks in between. Each stuffed chair has an occupant.

"As we all know, FMD, or Foot and Mouth Disease, had a very negative effect on our investments in South American beef production." Boris surveys the serious expressions, the frowns and nods. "The market plummeted as nations closed their doors to exports." A pause for effect. "I'm pleased to report that our decision to be proactive as regards this occurrence is now paying off nicely." Heads raise, weak chins stick out. "Our groups total share investment in the companies most affected by this crisis increased tenfold in the interim, at a fraction of the cost of the initial investment put at risk by FMD concerns." Some sage nods now, glances at their co-investors.

"As you recall, we reported that the European and Asian authorities agreed to reopen their markets provided certain infrastructure components were put in place to safeguard production standards. These components were financed internationally, and purchased from a variety of specialty manufacturers. Many of those manufacturers happen to be owned by our network of subsidiaries. As a result of these activities our return has surpassed fifty percent."

He pauses long enough to allow the tight smiles and congratulatory glances to circulate around the table. He goes on, and a few charts and financial reports later the group is almost giddy. Boris handles a couple of questions from the few whose ego requires they try to show some understanding. Then the business part of the New York meeting ends. They all file past.

As they make their way to the private elevator that will deliver them to the private underground parking and their limo's, Boris stands nearby. Each favors him, their employee, the one they choose to manage their wealth, with a smile, a small word, perhaps even a touch on the arm or shoulder. He absorbs it stoically, but still knows its high praise from this group.

"Good job, Boris."

"Thank you, Senator."

21

Albany County Jail

Broner's new attorney enters the interview room. The man is of medium height, with a crisp white shirt and pressed black suit. Sharp dark eyes, mid-fifties. A five foot eight inch version of Basil Rathbone. He shows no emotion as he enters the prison meeting room, sits down, back so straight it doesn't touch the chair, and looks into Jason Broner's hard face.

"So what are you going to do to help me?" demands Broner.

The man purses his lips and regards Broner for a moment. Broner shifts impatiently in his chair. The slightest hint of a smile flickers across Eli Massry's otherwise emotionless face. He leans forward, into Broner's space, folds his hands on the table, in Broner's space. His eyes don't leave Broner's.

"I think of you as scum," he lets the words hang in the air. "Filth," another pregnant pause. "If I were the prosecutor I'd want the death penalty for you," another small smile. "Unfortunately, there are worse than even you. Those are the ones I am truly after. If you can be useful to me in that pursuit, I will be useful to you. If I decide there is nothing here for me, for my hunt, or if you try to play me, you will not see me again, much to Mr. Chase's chagrin. Now tell me what you think you have, so I know if I've wasted my time coming here today."

Broner lets out a nervous laugh. Not what he expected from his new counsel. "You've got balls little man."

Massry sits back up straight, the thin lipped smile wider now, hands folded easily on his lap.

"My balls will walk out of here with me today, tough guy." He starts ticking points off on his fingers. "You were witnessed killing in cold blood a model citizen, a government employee, a family man, a veteran." That thin smile again. "Your looking at life inside a place designed for misery. Not to mention the playmates. So, have another laugh. You won't have many more chances. I'll be going." He rises to leave.

"Hold on," Broner loses the sneer, now a desperate look on his pockmarked face. "You don't know what I've got."

The suited man pauses and glances back at Broner, a look of mild interest on his face.

"I know who ordered the hit," Broner's eyes are wide now, hands stretching the cuffed wrists as he reaches toward Massry, pleading. "He doesn't know I know his name, he thinks I might be able to ID his man that set it up, but I know who he is." Broner takes a breath. "I need to get something for that," he emplors. "They'll kill me."

Massry takes a minute to inspect Broner, the upraised hands begging, the eyes pleading.

"You want freedom, you want witness protection," Massry is slowly nodding his head up and down, lips pursed. "To get that would mean that you provide evidence sufficient to build a case against those that hired you, strong enough to get a conviction. You will have to provide testimony, and because of this your life would have to be in jeopardy."

He lets this sink in.

"If your hit was contracted by a jealous husband or a small time loan shark, you don't qualify. Understand. I'm here because your court appointed counsel seems to think you've got a big fish to fry, and that the fish is part of a bigger organization, one Mr. Chase doesn't want to cross. One that I do. If this is not the case, then, once again, I'll be going."

Broner's back straightens as he leans towards Massry, willing him not to leave.

"Look, I'm not a cop. I can't make a case. What I've got is the name of the guy who ordered the hit. I don't know why he ordered it. I do know that he's very careful, has money and guns working for him, and a good cover. A big job on Wall Street. So, cards on the table, I've got a name, and I can testify he ordered the hit. Enough or not?"

Massry turns back towards Broner. "That depends on the name, and whether you can support your testimony with evidence, proof."

"Look, I'm not a lawyer either, but I've been around, and I think what I have can be backed up."

"The name?"

"Have we got a deal?" Broner pleads. Massry looks at the camera on the wall.

Eli Massry produces a pen and note pad from an inside pocket. "Write down the name," as he pushes them across the table. Broner takes the pen and rips off the top sheet of the pad. He leans over the paper and scribbles. He folds the paper and slides it back across the table.

The pen and notepad go back into the inner pocket. Massry picks up the paper, unfolds it, glances at it, then back at Broner. He refolds the paper and slips it into the same pocket as the pen and pad.

"We have a deal."

22

Ballyhinch

After the drive to Boston and the all night flight to Shannon Yvette and I are pretty tired by the time we pull the hire car into the driveway of the bungalow outside Ballyhinch on Ireland's west coast. Although the cottage is a rental we've stayed here several times in the past, and it feels like being home. Any sleep managed on the flight was, as usual, not too satisfying. Even though we've essentially been up for the past twenty hours, we decide to try and beat the jetlag by staying up, going to the shop for some groceries, then puttering around the place until it's time to shower and dress for dinner. Now we're comfortably settled in one of the traditional pubs off the towns narrow lanes. There's a long wooden bar topped with stained glass separations every few stools, finely crafted back bar filled with spirits, an open eating area and snugs on both ends, wall sconces providing just enough light. We have a table along the wall.

"You know, if you don't like those we won't pay for them. Send them back."

I'm referring to the two empty platters in front of Yvette. The larger had contained over a dozen steamed mussels, complete with a creamy white wine sauce. She'd scooped the sauce up with a soup spoon once the mussels were fully dispatched, then turned her attention to the plate of buttered crab claws, which were now gone as well.

"No," she says. "I don't want to embarrass anyone. Are you through picking at those ribs?" I've made just as short work of the potato and leek soup, which I followed with a rack of pork ribs. 'Comfort food'.

The dark wood gleams in the candlelight, and the low chatter from the other tables creates a comfortable mood. I'm enjoying a

Guinness while my sister has a white wine. I'm thrilled to see a big man with big hair and a guitar in his hands take his place on a stool along the wall near us.

"How are you folks tonight?" he smiles.

"Just fine, glad to see you." I really am glad to see him. In a lower voice I say to Yvette, "Being in the west of Ireland is like going back in time to me. Life just seems simpler, more straightforward."

"You'd never see this in New York," she agrees. "There'd be amps, speakers, a mic. Probably a cover charge."

"The music suits my mood more, too. There's nothing like a singer with a guitar." The man has a strong clear voice and seems to know every song ever written. No cheat sheets or search engine, he just knows the words and chords, everything from Guy Clarke and Bob Dillon to Tommy Fleming and Luke Kelly.

I catch Yvette looking at me, smiling.

"What's up?"

"It's just good to see you relaxed, happy. The past couple of weeks have been rough," her eyes drift away, then come back to mine. "Violence and loss. Anger and accusation. I'm proud of you, the way you were able to deal with it all. You've come a long way."

I pause for a moment and reflect back on those endless days of therapy.

"They said I was probably stronger when they were done with me than I was before."

"They also said it would be highly unlikely that you would ever test that strength," she reminds me. "You certainly didn't look for it, but you were tested anyway." She squeezes my hand. "And you've done well."

I reach over and put my hand over hers.

"Thanks, sis. Here we only have to listen to the waves and the birds, find our center again," my eyes go back to the singer with the guitar. "I'm looking forward to it. Peace at last," I squeeze her hand.

Get a squeeze back.

* * *

I wake out of a deep sleep. We were beat by the time we got back from the pub. My throat feels scratchy. I glance at the bedside clock and see its about 1 AM. I decide to go downstairs to the kitchen for a bottle of water. I pull on my sweats and crocks as quietly as I can. Yvette is usually a light sleeper, even with the day we've had, and I don't want to wake her. Her room is just down the hall, so I tiptoe to the top of the stairs.

As I head down the darkened hall I can see the back garden shine, bathed in moonlight. The front door faces the bottom of the stairs, with translucent glass panels at the top and bottom. Enough moonlight comes through for me to leave the stair light off, taking it careful, holding tight the bannister, eyes on the stairs. I look up after the bottom step. My breath catches in my throat. My blood runs cold.

Two shadowy silhouettes crouch outside the front door.

The sharp snap of the lock severs my only barrier to this nightmare. The door begins to swing open. The menace of the shadowy shapes morph into a real gun barrel advancing through the partial opening, and then the hand holding it.

I hear myself scream as some ancient instinct surfaces. I plant my foot and swivel at the hip, the roundhouse kick lands just below the handle, slamming the door into the gun hand of the man coming through it. I hear a muted cry as the pistol drops to the rough mat at my feet. I drop too, picking up the gun as the door bounces back open. Only feet away in the shadowy light, so close I could touch him, a man holds his hand, cursing. A second man, gun in hand, is struggling to get past him.

A shot explodes. I feel the bullet go by, smashing the masonry wall behind me. With one arm covering my head I raise the pistol, point it blindly towards the men, and jerk the trigger until all I hear is the click of the firing pin on an empty cylinder.

And Yvette screaming my name.

23

Somewhere in Northern Virginia

The cell had started ringing at 87, but the man really wanted the burn the pull-ups would leave him with so he did thirteen more. Quickly. He needed it. He dropped from the bar and grabbed the phone in one motion.

"Bobo," he answers as he drapes a towel around his neck.

"Boss, its Reid."

"What's up?" He hears Reid take a breath and some papers shuffle as he starts toweling off.

"Lot of the usual traffic, but this one guy has come up twice now. I haven't seen him before, didn't know he was on your list," Reid lets it hang a moment, goes on. "First time he came up as a witness to the murder of an investigator with NYSDA. That was two weeks ago."

Agricultural investigator. Terror, money laundering, blackmail?

"What category?" Bobo's list covered all sorts. Agents, former contacts, enemies, retired ops like him.

"Family," Reid replies. The category with only one name active.

"Who is it?" but Bobo knows.

"John Mann." Bobo still stiffens slightly as Reid continues. "Seems he got permission pretrial to take a short vacation he and his sister had planned to Ireland."

"OK," where's this going, Bobo wonders, getting annoyed.

"Well, it happened last night, the local Garda are calling it a home invasion, no link to any criminal or paramilitary groups they've found. Two guys, both armed, broke into the rental Mann and his sister were staying in."

Bobo catches his breath, drops the towel. No longer annoyed. Guilty worry.

"What happened?"

"Here's the funny thing. Seems Mann got a hold of one of their guns. Got one of them in the heart. The other bled out from a round in the throat."

Max Bobo holds the phone away from him and looks at it for a second. He puts it back to his ear.

"John Mann did that?"

24

Saint Lawrence Seaway, Thousand Islands

The houseboat is forty feet long with two inboard motors, a living area on the first deck that has a head and shower, bedroom, kitchen/dining area, and bridge. There's also a bridge up top. The top deck is a flat area, almost the length and width of the boat, covered with indoor/outdoor carpet. On the first deck, at the prow of the boat there's a sitting area and a barbecue grill. At the rear there's a small area that allows access to the ladder up top, as well as the area below accessing the engine compartment. The whole thing sits on two pontoons.

"Robert, I can't believe we're doing this." A light rain falls. The river became choppy when they left the shelter of the Gananoque marina.

Jurga's nervous being on the boat, although the St. Lawrence is still fairly calm. They're heading east, both of them stand at the inside bridge, matching the markers they pass with the ones on the map.

"Whatever is in that case must be evil, Jurga. Why else go through all this to get it out of Canada? Whoever they are, nothing can tie it to them. It's all on us."

"How long was it in our garage?"

They're moving along the channel on the Canadian side of the Islands. If they were on the other side, near the American coast, they would have to be wary of the wake caused by the large cargo vessels that work their way west to the Great Lakes on a continuous basis during the seasons when the St. Lawrence is ice-free.

"We have to stay on the Canadian side of this line on the map," Jurga is acting as navigator. The line was the border.

"Canadian and American Customs Officers prowl these waters,"

Robert said. "They track every boat that leaves one shore and docks at the other."

The river is immense, and the 1,000 plus Islands are a patchwork of channels, bays, and coves.

"There's food in the cooler, Robert, if you're hungry. You didn't eat any breakfast."

"No, thank you." They each have a gym bag with clothing, a cooler and the holdall. That was all they brought.

"There it is," Jurga looks up from the map, pointing.

"At least the dock's empty. It doesn't look like there's anyone around. I'll pull as close as I can, you jump off and tie us up."

As Jurga finishs securing the pontoon boat to the dock Robert appears with the holdall containing the suitcase. They follow the path toward the middle of the island. Five minutes later they're back. In no time they cast off and are back in the channel.

"We have to spend the night on one of two nearby islands," Robert says, thinking out loud. "We're to choose one with no other occupants if we can. Shouldn't be hard, not many around. We spend the night. If we get no further instructions, we can leave in the morning."

They motor on for about a mile.

"There it is," says Jurga. "It won't do. There's a powerboat tied up, and a houseboat like this one."

The power boat, about twenty four feet long, was berthed on one side of the dock, although it looked like they might be packing up to head home. On the other was a houseboat rental very much like theirs, with the same rental phone number emblazoned across the upper deck.

"The speedboat may be leaving shortly, but the houseboat looks like its here for the night." The men, in their twenties and thirties, were visible on the top deck, some sitting on lawn chairs, and some standing, but all with large cans in their hands.

"They look like they've been at it awhile, probably finish early. Let's try the next one."

The third island was further south toward the American shore and about half a mile back west. It had a small cove on the lee side that was empty, as was the cove on the north side. They choose the south side due to the protection from the wind, and settle in, hoping there will be no further instructions.

It's a gorgeous fall day, with bright sunshine and clear blue water, and a comfortable vessel under them.

"Will this be the end of it, Robert?" They're sitting inside on the sofa bed, staring absently at the river.

"I pray to God that it is, Jurga. I pray to God."

25

Ballyhinch

"I'm OK," I take a sip of my Guinness. "Look, I'm as surprised as you are, but I guess I'm handling stress a lot better. They said I was good to go at the clinic, but nobody ever knows for sure." We're back in the pub.

"It's sure being tested now, in spades." Yvette puts her glass down and looks at the newspaper on the bar in front of her. The sun is bright beyond the half curtained windows, the air full of muted conversation and occasional laughter offset by the clatter of silver, coffee cups and pint glasses. "You know, you are very lucky. Ireland's laws are in the process of changing, but essentially a homeowner that kills intruders goes to jail in this country."

"Better hope the news stays local. If Fendrick sees that headline he'll lock me up."

"Looks like a sunny day, have to take advantage of it. You never know here on the coast when you'll get another."

"So, you're off to the Cliffs of Moher?"

"Yeah. If the weather holds I can wrap it up today." She sighs as she looks over at me. "What are you going to do? Sure you can't come to France with me?"

"Greene was pretty adamant. Fact is, I sorta feel like heading home. That peace and quite we talked about last night seems farther away right now. Maybe I'll try the Adirondacks.".

"I remember when I first moved and found that house in Center Square. The Museum was just a short walk away."

"The closest I got was the parking lot."

"It was amazing. Wildlife, a whole section on birds. They have dioramas of the early Indian tribes. Even life sized mock ups of their shelters, their longhouses."

She stares into space. As I look at her I realize how beautiful my sister is. She turns to me, excited.

"There's a glade or a glen reproduced there. Trees and a pond, filled with wildlife. Let's see, there's a fox, a wolf, something like a lynx. Deer. Oh, and right in front of it all is a life size moose! It's hard to believe how big those things are. I think you'd really like that."

"I'm sure I would. Right now, though, I think I'll head for the real thing. If you finish up here today, will you head over to the cave shoot?"

"I guess so, especially if you're anxious to get back."

"I just don't need the confusion. I'll check with Greene and then head up to the mountains for some fishing."

"You sure? Your OK?"

"I'm fine. I can use the peace and quite. And the safety."

26

Saint Lawrence Seaway

It's a perfect fall day on the St. Lawrence. A chill bite in the air does nothing to take away from the beauty around them. The bright sky is enhanced by the occasional white fluff of cloud. The cool woodland around the dock is punctuated by the cries of migratory birds, heading south. The blue water as it swirls with the current and eddies proves hypnotic.

Jurga feels a quiet peace for the first time since the letters began to arrive. She hadn't looked for it, nor had she expected it. The combination of colors, smells, and sounds tricks her soul, and she's in a place she never expected to get back to, ever. Robert comes up behind her and places a comforting hand on her shoulder. He puts his arms around his wife. She drops her eyes, bows her head, pressing it against his comforting form.

"It's time to go."

Robert walks to the end of the dock as the clear waters laps the pilings. As he unties the rope and prepares to castoff he hears a faint boom. He glances at the sky over the northeast tip of the island. An oily cloud of black smoke is filling the horizon. The contrast with the beauty of the day couldn't be more sinister.

"Jurga, come. Look."

She sees the plume. Her eyes open wide with fear.

"Quickly, we must get out of here." They finish up, start the engines and pull away from the protected cove and into the river proper.

It becomes clear that the smoke is coming from the easternmost of the islands they explored the previous day, and from what they can see appears to be coming from the area where the lagoon and dock are.

They approach in a wide semicircle, not actually getting any closer, but positioned to see into the lagoon. As it comes into view terror grips their hearts. It's apparent that there's been an explosion. The smoke plume is the result of burning piles of debris, and floating pyres of burning gas and oil.

"We'll go a little closer. We must see if there is anyone we can help."

Robert navigates the boat upwind and approaches the flaming scene. The burning flotsam and oily black smoke are like a scene from a war, the shimmering of the flames against the green of the island and the blue of the sky a hellish intrusion. The smell is what shakes them. Not just gas, oil, wood and plastic. Flesh. Blown and burned to the waterline, the hull has sunk near the dock, while the rest of the carnage is being caught up in the current and pulled out of the lagoon, disappearing to the east.

"What could have caused such a terrible accident?" Jurga utters.

"I don't think it was an accident," Robert replies through clenched teeth. "I think that was supposed to be us."

Jurga looks at him in horror. "So, now what? They'll find out it wasn't us that died in the explosion. Will they come for us again?"

Robert's voice is low, somber, and angry. "There is no hope for our dear parents, I'm afraid. They never intended to spare them. But, our children, we must have hope, somehow for them. We're going to have to find a way to save them. For now, let's head away. There is nothing to be done for those unfortunate men, and being here when the officials arrive will raise questions I'm not sure yet how to answer."

27

Somewhere in Northern Virginia

"That's pretty much all of it, Max."

Reid takes another sip of his coffee. The small restaurant is starting to fill up. Reid and Max Bobo have their usual seat at the small table at the back of the room. They wouldn't stand out immediately. If you watched them, however, you'd notice they both had military bearing and a swimmers muscular physique. You'd also notice that Bobo is possibly thirty years older than Reid.

Here they have some privacy. The table is situated so they can each see the front door and the street beyond the windows. There is a door nearby that says 'Employees Only' that leads to the rear alley or up the stairs to the roof. These things are second nature to them. Reid has given Max the weekly update on his list of persons of interest.

"Anymore on John Mann?" Bobo's question piques Reid's curiosity.

"You think there's something there?"

"You never know. I don't believe in coincidences. Seems odd that he should witness a murder and a couple of weeks later be the object of an event."

"Christ, Max, the 'event' happened four thousand miles away. What makes you think they're connected?"

Bobo refills his cup from the carafe, takes another forkful of egg, looks at Reid. "How would you do it?"

Reid's eyes narrow. He butters a piece of toast. He doesn't look at Bobo.

"You have a connection with Mann. He's on the list."

Bobo nods. "He was married to my niece."

"The one that died in the fire? With the daughter?"

Bobo nods again. "He blamed himself, had a breakdown. Wasn't his fault at all, he'd been trying to deal with an impossible situation." Bobo looks at Reid. "It was a bad time for him. I didn't think he had what it took to get over something like that. I wasn't too kind at the time."

Reid eats his toast while Max stares into his coffee.

"She was my brother's daughter. Our mother died when we were young. The old man couldn't cope. He drank and beat us. I took off for the Corps when I was sixteen. My brother stayed. He didn't turn out to be much of a father, either. Put a gun in his mouth when Jenny, that's my niece, was fifteen. When she got pregnant Mann thought he was doing the right thing, but it was never going to work. I'd just come back from a rough mission, had no sympathy for these candy assed civilians, and showed it. Never was any good with the grief thing."

"Roger that," says Reid, with a smirk. "So, what? You looking for some way to make up for that? Does this guy really need your kind of help?"

Bobo looks at his comrade and smiles.

"I don't know. It would be nice if he did, though, wouldn't it?"

Reid just shakes his head. "War horses."

28

Manhattan

Boris stares out the window but his thoughts are nowhere near the breathtaking view. His target is so much bigger than Manhattan.

The package is now mine. The plan goes forward. The witness still lives. Pavel will solve this problem the Irish couldn't. Back-up just in case. Can't let anyone get the scent, can't have anything go wrong. Too close. Push back the FBI and JD, cool things down. Only need a little time.

29

Albany, New York

"Tomorrow, if that's OK with you," says Agent Greene.

I'd asked if he needed me for anything before I went up north fishing. He said the US Attorney wanted to take a deposition. I'm in the kitchen, next to the phone.

"Something else I should tell you about," I feel I ought to fill him in on Ireland. Wouldn't do to have him find out about it third hand. He seems to take it well enough. I suppose after all the years he's had in with the FBI it would be hard to rattle him.

"There's something I should tell you about, too."

"What's that?"

"Had a call, from a guy says he knows you, wanted to know what was going on with the Dixon investigation."

"Who?"

"Max Bobo," Greene says, the respect in his voice evident. "How's he know you?"

"He was my wife's uncle. Is. Anyway." I'm flustered at the mere mention of his name. The whole time Jenny and I were married I heard about uncle Max and the heroic things he'd been up to. His time in 'Nam as a recon marine, whispered work with the CIA. Homicide detective in the City, then head of the Anti-Terror Group when it was set up after 9/11. Last I heard he was back into black ops.

"I only met him one time, at the funeral. It was all a blur, but I recall that he didn't seem to like me too much. I remember Yvette had a go at him."

"Your sister had a go at Max Bobo? I do have to meet your sister. Let her know I'm a friend, OK?"

"What did he want? What did you tell him?"

"Being former law enforcement, and being Max Bobo, hell he could still have a badge, I told him what I knew. He was curious about any leads we had on Dixon's killer, not Broner, whoever hired him. Of course, we don't have much, although Broner has a new attorney. The guy he has is a guy he can't afford. There is some back channel talk of Broner looking for a deal if he gives some people up. So far nothing concrete, though."

"Anything else?"

"Well, yeah. He knew about Ireland, told me. Said he didn't believe in coincidences."

"What's that mean?"

"It means he's worried about you."

"Should I be worried?"

"I don't know. Guys like Max get paid to worry. They want the action. He's sort of retired now, from what they tell me."

Greene tells me where to be next day, and what time. I tell him where I'll be going as soon as we're done with the US attorney, and how to contact me. Again, I find myself looking forward to some peace and quiet.

30

Pavel

The sunglasses disguise the deadly eyes, so the khaki pants and NASCAR themed jacket and hat give the little man an almost comical look.

"Could I have your passport and license, please?"

The Hertz clerk is blindly efficient, as expected. It had been a short train ride from the City to Kingston.

"Thank you, Mr. Brown. Please sign here, here, and here. And next to the box you checked, that you want all the additional insurance."

"These are your copies, sir. Space number 23. The keys are in the ignition. I hope you enjoy your stay in America."

***

Forty five minutes later the medium sized Ford rental drifts into the right hand exit lane. He crosses the bridge and pays the toll, the late morning sun reflecting off his mirror sunglasses . The well-signed tree lined highway takes him to an address in Connecticut he'd looked up on the internet the prior day. The stripped log, low slung building crouches grandly on the far side of an acre size parking lot. Pavel nudges the Ford between two pick-up trucks. He stands outside the car and stretches for a minute before approaching the glass double doors, flanked on each side by a stuffed black bear. As he enters and feels the welcome coolness he's assailed by the sight of more stuffed bear, dear, and moose heads on the wall over the long glass cased counter.

"Can I help you, sir?" The salesperson can't be more than twenty, with bits of metal in both ears, tongue, upper lip and eyebrows.

"I'm looking for a dual taser/stun gun." The kid nods excitedly, apparently familiar, and delighted, with this lethal bit of technology. As

77

the clerk fumbles with keys to open a nearby display case Pavel takes a look around the store. There's about twenty people wandering the aisles, but due to the floor size the place looks empty. The kid pops up in front of him, the prize held in both open hands.

"There's roughly 50,000 volts on offer," he carefully exhibits the pair of dart tipped wires. "Accurate to about fifteen feet." He slowly turns the taser as he speaks. "Law enforcement likes this weapon because the effect on the target is instant submission, the inability to perform any activities involving the voluntary nervous system for up to five minutes."

"There've been some break-ins around my neighborhood," 'Brown' says. "That may not disable a burglar long enough for the police to arrive."

"We recommend spare cartridges. You can zap 'em again if you need to. That's what ordinary citizens like about it."

Pavel moves his head up and down in appreciation.

"I'll take it," he reaches for his wallet. "Let me have spare air cartridges, too."

31

Prehistoric Cave, Southern France

They'd been in the narrow passageway for about a half hour. They could hear faint noises made by the other teams in the area, although it was impossible in the subterranean recesses to tell what direction the sounds came from. Some could be identified by the language spoken, but where they were was anyone's guess.

"Shit," Mark cursed as he banged his head again on the uneven rock surface. Yvette couldn't help but laugh. The intern she'd been assigned was over six feet tall with brown sandy hair and dark eyes. He was bright and industrious, very serious, a little clumsy, and took these bangs as personal insults.

"Mark, we'll have to get you some head protection. France is a big rugby nation, maybe one of those tight fitting headguards?"

"Sorry about the swearing."

The light was poor and then some, and even with the strobe the passage was so narrow it was almost impossible to illuminate the subject, a plain looking red mark, almost a dot. It wasn't just any red mark. The people Yvette was working with told her that this particular 'red mark' could be twenty five thousand years old. According to their theory it was painted in this narrowest part of the cave because the acoustics at this point allowed echoes to reverberate through this vast underground network of tunnels and passages. The sound produced was very like the prehistoric animals they hunted. When the team treated her to an audial sample, the resulting primal roars and barks raised the hair on her neck, and her blood rushed as she struggled with the fight or flight response.

"Mark, I'm going to stay past the normal quitting time. I've got to get these shots right, and I can't take a chance on messing up the schedule for the rest of the team. I wish I could tell you to go ahead with the others, but the rule is not to be in here alone. Sorry."

"No prob. I don't mind at all, I need the experience."

A footfall sounded from around the corner of the passage where it led into the main tunnel. The familiar figure in khaki with flaming red hair entered the work area with a smile on his broad face. Dr. James Sullivan was the senior archeologist for the project.

"Can't wait for my filet mignon, a lovely glass of red wine, perhaps a soccer match on the TV in the lounge," he teased. Yvette laughed.

"Hi, Jim. Guess you heard I'm staying late to finish up here."

"Couldn't help but rub it in a little."

"Go ahead and make fun. I'm not a big red meat or soccer fan. I'll be just as happy getting this lighting right," she smiled.

"I understand completely. I'll let your driver know. Don't work too late, though. Tomorrow's a busy day, too."

***

It was well over two hours later when Yvette and Mark exited the cave. They followed the system of reflective markers so they didn't get lost in the labyrinthine tunnels. LED lights with motion detectors were placed along the way to limit the need to use flashlights. The lights were on the left entering, the right returning, to help the team members keep from getting lost. Even so, spending many hours underground was disorienting.

"Mark, take a breath of that fresh air. Isn't it wonderful?"

"Yeah. It's like a wash for the lungs."

The French countryside was quiet and cool. In the distance fields filled with wheat as far as the eye could see changed color and shape with the action of the slight breeze as shadows began to lengthen. The hills behind would block the sun soon and a chill already filled the air. Dusk was upon them.

"I don't see Alain anywhere, do you?"

Yvette was on her tiptoes sheltering her eyes from the sun, which was low in the west, as she surveyed the parking area and the narrow farm road that led away from the protected site. The rented van was parked about twenty feet away, but was clearly empty.

"I don't mind the extra time, but now it's done I want a shower, a meal and a rest. I hope we're not waiting around here for long," Mark said as he kicked at a stone.

They walked over to the van, which was unlocked. They got in. A few minutes later they saw Alain come down the hill, holding his cell phone.

"He might have been up there looking for a signal," Yvette suggested.

He approached the vehicle, his attention on his mobile screen. He looked at Yvette for what seemed a moment too long. Alain got behind the wheel, started the van and drove them away from the cave, never saying a word.

32

Suburbs, Albany, New York

The home was set back on a double lot, a pine log fence along the front, a driveway going around the side to the two car garage. The yard was landscaped. There was an attractive stone façade. Greene pulled into the driveway and walked up the path to the front door. He could hear someone approaching as soon as he rang the bell.

An attractive woman in her early forties, stylish in a simple black dress, opened the door.

"Mrs. Dixon?" She nodded, a curious expression on her face. "I'm Agent John Greene with the FBI," he held his credentials where she could see them. "My condolences on your loss." She nodded again. "I was wondering if you could spare a few minutes to answer a couple of questions. It could help in our investigation."

Looking a tad confused Julia Dixon showed Greene into a modest living room with several comfortable looking chairs and a flat screen TV. Greene sat, and after refusing Mrs. Dixon's offer of tea or coffee, so did she.

"I'm afraid I don't understand, Agent Greene. I thought you caught the murderer, that he was identified by that terrible man, the witness."

Greene frowned and cocked his head.

"Why do you say the witness is a terrible man?"

"Detective Fendrick told me he killed his wife and daughter."

Greene didn't know where to start.

"I'm sorry, Mrs. Dixon, but the detective had no right telling you that. It was unsubstantiated and turned out to be totally false. Mr. Mann lost his wife and daughter in a tragic fire, but he had no hand in it."

Julia Dixon's hand went to her mouth. "Oh, my. I feel awful. Ever since Ken's funeral I've been thinking terrible things about that poor man. Why would the detective say that about him if he didn't know it was true?"

"I don't really know, Mrs. Dixon. He jumped to some conclusions, emotions were high. Really, there's no excuse, though. I'm glad we cleared that up, but that's not what I came to talk to you about. You're right that we have the man we believe pulled the trigger, but we now have good reason to believe that it wasn't a botched robbery."

"What do you mean?" Her brow furrowed and her eyes sharpened again as she looked at Greene.

"We believe that someone hired Jason Broner to kill your husband."

She gasped and sat back. Her mouth dropped open. "But who? Why?"

"That's what I'm hoping you can help us with. Did your husband have any enemies, maybe someone he prosecuted?"

She looked off to the side, forehead knit, then slowly shook her head.

"Not that I know of. He never said anything, anyway. He didn't really talk much about his job at home. Much of it was sensitive. The most he'd do is joke around some, like riddles. I suppose you'd have to ask them at work. As for outside of work, I'd have to say no. Ken was well liked by everybody. He was always helping people. He had a big heart, a guiding sense of fairness. No, I can't think of anyone."

"Did he have a home office, a computer, or files? Something that might show if he was working on an investigation that might be significant?"

"Yes, there's a room down the hall. You're welcome to take a look. His laptop is in there."

Greene followed her down the hall to a small, neat office. It seemed well organized. As he looked through the files the material all seemed related to household or personal items. He looked through the laptop, but found nothing of interest. Mrs. Dixon agreed to one of his techs dropping by to take a deeper look.

"OK. Thank you, Mrs. Dixon, that's all for now. If you think of anything please give a call. My number is on that card."

"Agent Greene, is this your case now?"

"Yes. The FBI has jurisdiction when a state official or law enforcement is intentionally murdered."

"I hope you'll keep me informed. Mr. Fendrick apparently forgot to do that where the facts were involved." Greene smiled to himself at Fendrick's demotion in her eyes from 'detective' to 'mister'.

She showed him to the door. She was still standing there as he drove away.

33

Adirondack Mountains

The drive always served as a balm for my soul. I entered the Adirondack Park, over six million acres, more than the largest National Parks combined. Within it's borders there were over 10,000 lakes, some 30,000 miles of rivers and streams. The rivers and watersheds appeared first, followed by the lower hills, the foothills, and then the roads were winding through tall peaks. Pine trees threw off a scent that filled my lungs with fond memories. Campfires and warm sleeping bags. Morning chill followed by the smell of fresh coffee and bacon. Logs burning.

The deposition had gone OK, I thought. Greene was a much more comfortable person to work with then Fendrick had been. He didn't say anymore about Max. Maybe he'd satisfied himself and moved on.

I parked the truck in the small glade and walked the hundred yards or so to the log cabin. There was no telephone or cell coverage here. No electricity. Solar panels and a propane canister provided what amenities there were. There was a woodpile and a fireplace, of course. Kerosene lamps kept the darkness at bay after sunset, which came early among these peaks. I got a small blaze going in the fire ring, ate the sandwich I'd brought and washed it down with a beer. I realized how tired I was. I put it down to all that had been going on, and longed for my bed and a good nights sleep. Breakfast in the morning, and then down to the fast flowing river for some relaxation with my fly rod.

34

Adirondack Mountains

Pavel sat in the trees and watched his prey putter around the cabin. He'd parked a half a mile further up the road and walked to this point. The bugs weren't too bad. After about an hour he felt he had the feel of the place, a sense of rhythm.

He walked back to his car and drove the fifteen minutes it took to reach his motel. When he got to the motel he activated the Taser. He got on line with the barcode from the device and the last four digits from the long dead Donald Brown's social security number. When he got his activation code he opened the safety cover. The first digit was 4. He pulled the trigger four times. He closed the safety cover and reopened it and repeated the process with each of the other digits. The green light came on.

35

Adirondack Mountains

The night mist was swirling upward into the pines as the heat of the rising sun pulled it higher and higher. Pavel wore his protective sunglasses, not waiting for the sun to break over the hills. The path was damp, dew on the bushes that lined the trail, a faint chill in the air. He gave the cabin a wide berth, although he could see the fishing gear lined up on the deck table, could smell coffee percolating. He didn't have far to go. The trail wound around an outcropping on the right, the junction gradually coming into view straight ahead. Heavy branched conifers lined both sides of the trail. On the left a path dropped down to the river, and the canoe that sat on its bank. Just past the turnoff the original trail kept going along the ridge, past a large boulder. The assassin moved carefully behind this boulder, hidden from anyone headed down to the canoe but still able to step out behind them without being seen. Pavel waited with the patience of the hunter, breathing easy and relaxing his muscles, the Taser held easily in his two hands. Step out, aim, fire. Get the body into the water. Watch.

He heard the noise, all his senses instantly on high alert. Footsteps, clomp clomping to their fate. Pavel hunched lower as he heard Mann approach the junction, ready to noiselessly devour his prey. Almost, almost.

Something's wrong. Pavel can still hear the steps, but doesn't see Mann. Still crouched alongside the boulder, he looks over his right shoulder and sees Mann, five feet away but behind him now, continuing along the trail. If Mann looks over he'll spot Pavel, who remains motionless as Mann continues along the ridge line, quickly disappearing among the trees. Pavel moves around the boulder and stares after Mann. He crouches and follows carefully, moving from cover to cover, as the path winds along between trees and around boulders. He spots Mann occasionally, but can't get close enough for a clear shot. Pavel stays alert, but then he loses him.

The trail ahead straightens out. Reluctantly Pavel moves out from the cover of the trees. He treads cautiously.

'Thunk'

Down. To his left.

There's Mann. He's in the river. He's working his way out among the rushing waters using boulders as stepping-stones. Pavel stops at the rim, hunkers down for a good look at his target. Mann's now at a point almost mid-stream, the appliance sized rocks surrounded by white water. There he stands, jeans, white T-shirt and running shoes, a vest with his gear, a wicker creel low on his back. A rictal smile from the rim.

The talus-strewn slope is steep. Pavel checks that his belly pack is secure. He carefully crawls hand over foot onto the loose, rocky slope, and starts a slow descent to the waters edge. As he nears the bottom he too dislodges a rock. Clatter, clatter, 'thunk'. Mann had been absorbed with his fly rod and the gear on his vest, but looks up when he hears the noise, spotting Pavel in his NASCAR jacket and oversized sunglasses. Pavel's expression doesn't change as he points at his waist pack and makes picture-taking gestures with his hands.

He yells "Photos," but the word is drowned out by the roar of the river. Mann seems uncertain and looks around him. He's standing on a point of rock thirty feet from shore, surrounded by turbulent water. He hesitates and then appears to go back to preparing his rod. Pavel leaps from shore to the nearest boulder, then quickly hopscotches to a third. Mann catches this action, sees that he's being cut off from the shore. He slowly reaches behind him and pulls out a five inch fishing knife, holding it uncertainly. Pavel takes another jump. He's closed to around twenty feet from Mann. Another jump. Mann is starting to look worried, glances at the water at his feet. Last jump.

Pavel figures the distance at about twelve feet. There are still a couple of large rocks between them, but he's close enough. His pale fingers unzip the belly pack as the eyes behind the triple UV glasses take on a sexual excitement. With one motion Pavel removes the Taser and kneels on the uneven surface. After steadying himself with one hand, he braces his elbow on his knee, pulls back the safety, and uses both hands to aim.

Mann's eyes grow wide as he sees the device, unsure how to react. He crouches low and pulls the creel out in front of him. He slides as far down the rock as he can, but still his whole torso is exposed. There's a 'swoosh' as the air fills with confetti tags and the darts with their fifty thousand volts fly towards Mann.

Pavel sees him wince as one dart sticks in his arm. Then he sees the other dart stuck in Mann's creel. He steadies himself and sets to reloading. A quick glance sees Mann pull the dart from his arm, spot the one in the creel and look back up to see Pavel. Pavel is confident as he inserts another cartridge. Mann now understands what he's up against. As Pavel readies his second shot Mann pulls himself up to a crouch and starts swinging his fly rod, even though he can't reach Pavel. The tip of the rod whips the air two feet from Pavels face as he continues unfazed.

Mann frantically waves the flyrod – back and forth, in circles, up and down. Pavel can see the panic, can sense the end is coming soon. He steadies himself, calmly watching the gyrations Mann is creating with the rod. He takes his time as the man in front of him becomes more intent. Trying for the right timing he presses the trigger and the darts fly once more. Another 'swoosh'.

The erratic motion of the rod sends one of the darts off course. Mann stops waving the rod, but has no time to feel relief as Pavel calmly takes another shell by the sides and reloads, relishing this contest in which he has all the advantage.

In an instant he's loaded. A motion draws his attention back to Mann, he's surprised to see that he's leaped to another boulder, one within fly rod distance. Pavel pushes the safety off. Mann swings the tip of the rod at his face. The whip like tip lashes the protective sunglasses off, exposing his colorless eyes to the bright sunlight. Pavel flinches, one hand flies up to cover his eyes. The other, as it pulls back the safety mechanism, flexes. Two probes, designed to travel fifteen feet and penetrate two cumulative inches of clothing, explode directly into his thigh. The energy bursts last thirty seconds, during which the fifty thousand volts surge through Pavel's body. He vibrates like the high voltage wire he's become, a dark force having taken over his body and making it move in impossible ways. The burst feels like it will go on forever, but finally stops. Pavel is now a puppeteers doll with the strings cut, confetti whirling around him. The plastic gun drops and he tries to reach for it. His arms don't respond. His eyes alone reflect the horror as he slowly slides backwards off the rock. There's anger as his pained eyes shift to Mann, standing six feet away, disbelief on his own face. Pavel enters the water, helpless to move his limbs. The NASCAR jacked billows up around his disembodied head, slowly sinking as it floats downstream with the current, revolving on its green nylon lily pad.

Then he's gone.

36

FBI Offices, Albany, New York

"Mr. Bobo. How're you doing?" Bobo had the number for his direct line.

"Call me Max or Bobo, OK Greene?"

"Sure, …Bobo."

"Anything new?"

"Not really. I talked to Dixon's widow and his employer. Neither seems to know anything useful, but I'll follow up. Has to be some reason why someone wanted Dixon dead."

"I see," Bobo paused. "Look, I stopped by Mann's house. Nobody there. Any idea where they are?"

"The sister has a photo job in France right now, another week, I guess. We deposed him yesterday and he said he was heading up to that cabin he has in the mountains. Feeling the strain, I guess. Wanted to go fishing."

"He's on his own?"

"Far as I know. He didn't mention anyone else."

"Think that's wise? After the Ireland thing."

"Just a home invasion. Happens more and more. The economy, I guess. And the general lawlessness. No connection we can see. The guy just needs some time off."

"Hmm… Maybe I'll head up there. Try and get there around noontime. Maybe he'll have some fish for lunch. What are the co-ordinates?"

Greene looked at his phone. "I don't have co-ordinates. I've some directions I can give you. Then you're on your own."

"Give 'em to me. I'll plot a route. Thanks, Greene."

37

Mann's Camp

I'm not shaking as I walk back up to the camp, which surprises me. I'd pulled the dart out of the creel and another one out of my arm. He'd dropped his gun and the spare cartridge on the rock when he fell in. I picked them up as I worked my way unsteadily to the shore. Now I set them on the small table on the deck.

The little man in the ridiculous outfit had tried to kill me. It was me that was supposed to fall helpless into the fast current, unable to use my arms or legs as I slowly drowned. By the time my body was found it would have been battered by rocks. The two dart marks wouldn't have been noticed. A terrible accident. A movement catches my eye and I jump. A figure in jeans and a black t-shirt is walking up the trail from the road in. It takes a moment, but I recognize him and feel a jolt of fear. Max Bobo.

"Stay where you are! Don't come any closer." I put more confidence in my voice than I feel. "I have a shotgun inside the door."

The man stops and holds up his hands, smiling. "Easy John. It's me, Max."

"I know who you are. Looking for your little friend?"

"John, calm down," Max says quietly, a concerned look now crossing his tanned features. "I'm not here to hurt you. Tell me what's going on."

He slowly sits down in the grass, crosses his ankles. He places his hands on his knees where I can see them.

We stare at each other for a while, I don't know how long.

"Why are you here, Max?"

Max is perfectly still, sitting on the forest path like a college freshman on a campus green. His eyes never leaving mine.

"I called by the house in Albany and nobody was home. Greene told me you were up here, gave me directions."

"Why, Max?"

He slowly shakes his head, appreciating my concern.

"I'm worried about what's been going on. You being a witness, the thing in Ireland. Just a feeling, but I trust my feelings. Always have. Rarely wrong. Felt guilty about years ago, too. Not your fault. I was too tough on you. So here I am."

We study each other a while longer. I want to believe him. I do believe him.

I walk to where he sits and hold out my hand. He takes it and I can feel his strength as he effortlessly lifts himself to his feet.

"What little friend?" he asks

I force a smile.

"You would've been too late."

38

Manhattan

Boris calls Victor into the office. "When did Pavel check in?"

"Two hours ago. He was on a sat-phone in his car near the camp. He said he'd be back to us in less than an hour, when it was done."

Boris taps a pencil on the green blotter. "No word from him at all?"

"None."

"Did you set up the backup we talked about?"

"Yes. They're in position at a nearby landfill. Twenty minutes out."

"Make the call and send them in. If Pavel has been compromised I'm through with deception. Have them kill the witness. We'll handle the fall out. We don't need long. The FBI might suspect a connection to Broner, but they'll still have no proof. I'll chance it. I want John Mann dead."

"Yes, boss."

39

Albany County Correctional Facility

"I think we can be fairly confident that the Government will give immunity from prosecution to your accomplice, the tail. Will he submit to a deposition if that's the case?" Massry asks.

They were at the County Jail. Built in 1931 it was one of the largest facilities in the State with over four hundred sworn officers and civilian workers tending to the daily population of over eight hundred inmates. Located just outside the City of Albany it was about a two and a half hour drive from Manhattan. There was the option of video visitation, but Eli Massry preferred face to face, so they sat in one of the rooms reserved for attorney client consultations.

"Yeah, he will," Broner says.

"Tell me about the murder itself."

"OK," Broner takes a deep breath. "Well, like I said, I always map these things out pretty good. I knew from the tail that this guy Dixon worked in one of the towers, but parked in a lot over behind the big building across the street from the main mall. What he'd do is, he'd walk across this Plaza, cross the street, and go through the museum. Sometimes he'd come out right away, sometimes he'd take a while. My tail said he'd go into the museum and walk around the exhibits those times. It was better for me when he did that cause it gave the other folks going to the lot time to get out of there." Broner pauses, as if the re-creation is more effort than he can handle.

"What was the lot like?"

"His part was off the beaten track a little, I guess because he was a big shot. The place was pretty central, but there were trees, and the paths around the place had bushes along 'em. Basically, I waited until my tail called me on his throwaway to tell me it was a museum day, and then I walked over and hung around the paths. There's things there, Memorials like, for the wars, for firefighters, cops that have been killed. They have names on 'em. It was easy to hang around there and not stand out."

Massry looks up from the notes he's taking. "How long was he in the museum?"

"About a half hour."

"Then what?"

"He came along. I walked up behind him, waited 'til he got to a place in the lot where nobody could see us, called his name, shot him, took his stuff and legged it."

"But somebody did see you."

"No, not from where people should have been. This asshole must have been someplace else. Anyway, he saw me shoot the guy, take his watch, wallet and briefcase, and run off."

"Briefcase?"

"Yeah" Broner said. "Your friend from Brighton Beach wanted the briefcase."

40

Adirondack Mountains

Max stares at the remains of the device, shaking his head.

"What is it, Max?"

"I knew that something was up."

"How so?"

He shakes his head again, mouth tight, lips drawn in. He spreads his hands on the table and leans towards me.

"Look, that Ag guy was a hit, that was clear. Somebody takes out someone like that plays big. Then when the 'home invasion' happened in Ireland, it was clear that they played real big. International big. Those guys were too well armed to be housebreakers. And for what? Yvette's camera bag?"

Hard to argue. Also hard to comprehend when it's happening to you and you haven't a clue why. Max stands next to the scarred fillet table, still staring at the toy like plastic device I'd brought up from the river.

"And now this. C2. Supposed to look like an accident. Somebody would've fished your body out downstream, nobody would even know where it happened." He pauses and looks at me. "The thing I can't figure out, though, is how you beat the two armed guys in Ireland, and this duck. He had to be a pro. You say he looked like an albino?"

"Maybe. White hair, and his eyes were really strange."

"So, how'd you do it?"

"Oh," I pause and shrug my shoulders. "Well in Ireland I was just real scared, just did what I did. I was lucky. Here I was scared, too. I was also mad. And lucky."

Max looks down at the taser, then looks over at me, smiling.

"You're growing in the job, John. That's good. Luck doesn't hurt either, but you just can't count on it."

"What job is that, Max?"

"Staying alive."

We head down to the cars. Max had spotted a rental up the road and figures it must belong to the NASCAR guy. Max has a sat-phone in his car, along with some other gear he wants to have handy. Considering. Plan is to call the State Police and alert them there's a body in the river. Also to step up our own security.

We're almost to the cars, at the edge of the woods, when Max holds his hand up and squats. I do the same. At first I don't see anything, but when Max points up the road I see a reflection. Sunlight off a car windshield. As I look closer I can see a black garbed figure walking around it. It might be a truck or SUV.

Max shakes his head. "Shit. Can't break cover to get to the car and grab my gear." Suddenly Max has a pistol in his hand. "You really have that shotgun?"

"Yeah. Twelve gauge, and a box of shells. Hasn't been shot in a while."

"Run, don't walk, and get that shotgun. Then get out of the cabin. Hide somewhere and get ready to head for that canoe you've got. I'll meet you there."

I'm not mad now. Not feeling real lucky, either. I'm scared. Shitless. "What's going on, Max?"

"There're four of them, John. They've blocked the road, and they're coming in ready. If they were cops they would have driven right up. I don't like it. Get ready to fight, OK?"

My breathing is labored and my heart is racing, but somehow I manage to run back up the trail, which suddenly looks more like a tunnel. I get to the cabin and the only thought I can hold onto is to do exactly what Max says. The shotgun is hanging over the fireplace, and it takes me a few seconds to find the box of shells. It takes two tries to shove the box into my jeans cargo pocket.

When I get outside the clearing suddenly looks as long as a football field. My legs won't let me head across so I run behind the cabin. I just make it when there's a burst of automatic fire, splintering the corner of the cabin and the fir trees next to it.

I drop to the ground and am able to see the path through an opening in the concrete blocks that form the cabin's foundation. Four men in black, weapons at the ready, are advancing in a fanned out formation across the clearing, periodically firing bursts. I look at them, then at the shotgun. I haven't even loaded it yet. I look back their way. They're firing another burst when the one on my right lurches towards the others and goes down, blood spurting from under his armpit. It takes the others a moment to realize what happened, and then they re-form and sweep the right hand woods with automatic fire.

Apparently that moment is enough for Max to bail. He's suddenly at my side. He takes the shotgun from me, digs shells out of my cargo pocket, and loads the gun.

"They won't make anymore mistakes," he says. "Let's go."

I do what Max does, which is to crawl backwards down a small incline until we can crouch and run toward the river. I have a canoe and paddles there. The life jackets are in the cabin. I suppose that doesn't matter.

"Get in the front and get ready to paddle hard. I'll be on the run when I come back."

I try to hold the canoe steady in the water as Max takes the shotgun and disappears into the woods. I hear both barrels go off, followed by a volley of automatic gunfire. Max bursts out of the woods, throws the shotgun in, runs the canoe into the river and with a hand on each gunnel levers his body and rotates into paddling position. Then we're moving.

"That'll slow them down. Paddle hard but stay low."

We hug the shoreline for a bit and then head for the middle where the current will grab us. Being in the front, my job is to avoid the rocks that litter the stream by pulling the front of the canoe to one side or the other. The river is a palette of upriver and downriver 'V's and pillows.

Max's paddling is moving us faster than the current, so I can do the maneuvers that keep us off the rocks. The channel runs between large boulders where we hit the flume between them and ride fast. I look ahead and see a bend. If we can get there we'll have some cover.

When I chance a look back I wish I hadn't. Three men in black stand on the shore aiming at us.

A rock to my right splinters the air as a bullet ricochets off it. I drive my paddle into the raging water to set our course on a flume between two boulders as a splash on my left tells me they're getting the range. We hit the flume and fly through as another shot lands at the waterline, we start to slow. Fear gives me strength as I frantically put my back into the muscle tearing process of inching towards the current. Some of the boulders provide cover but I can hear the sound of the shots and the impact on rock. Max screams at me, "Go, go, go!"

I desperately fling the paddle forward, frantically dig it into the water, then pull it back with every ounce of strength and leverage I can summon. My lungs ache and it hurts to breathe. My arms are numb from the wet and cold, the paddle gripped so tightly that its now part of me. I can think of nothing, my brain overloaded with fear and the primal need to get away.

We make it to the current. The front of the canoe pulls forward as we straighten out and pick up speed even as it takes on water from the hole in the side. I paddle with the same desperation as we gain on the bend in the river, then after another 'V' and a pillow we make it around.

I feel like we're safe and want to slump over the bow, aching arms trailing in the cold water, but Max yells to keep going. Somehow I do. The river slows down and opens up as we pass steep cliffs on either side, thirty or forty feet high, covered with scrub growth. We sail past, the world quiet now. The roil of the narrows is behind us, as is the sound of the guns firing and the bullets ricocheting. Hawks are flying overhead, and the trees on the rim are full of birdsong.

"John," Max doesn't have to yell as loud now. "There's a small sandbar ahead to the right, the inside of the bend. Bring us around and I'll power us in."

I place my paddle in the water on the left of the bow holding the shaft above the throat, resting it on the gunnels and using downward pressure on the grip to leverage the canoe to the right. Max increases our speed and we cut across the current to the slip of sand. As we strike the spit I grab the painter, holding it to my chest as I stumble out of the boat and onto the sand, the slim bit of rope pulls against my efforts to hold it as the wet sand gives under my feet. Max drags the stern onto the sandbar and we both collapse. The sun shines down on us, two exhausted men and a shot-up canoe prostrate amidst the sparkling water, granite cliffs and towering pines.

In spite of the running I do, and Max being in his mid-sixties, he recovers before I do. He's on his feet, eyes searching the cliffs above us. "We need a plan," he announces, tearing a strip off his shirt. He ties a knot in it, and shoves it through the hole at the canoe's waterline. Ties it off on the inside so it's tight.

"There's an access point about two miles down. We can get out there."

Max shakes his head 'no'. "I saw that on my map. They'll be waiting for us there. We have to get out before then."

"I've been down this section a few times, Max. It's pretty much of a climb out until the launch."

"We're gonna have to climb out, then. We'll be sitting ducks if they see us coming, or if they come along the rim." He glances towards the top of the cliffs on either side. "They'd be on that side," he nods at the bank we came in on. "So, we have to climb out on the other side. Know of anyplace?" He's already pushing the canoe into the river. I don't believe I can move, my breath still comes in gasps as sweat drips onto my wet clothes. I roll to my knees, half walk, half crawl, and pull myself into the canoe, dropping into the bow. My bruised and aching knees take up their position again, as I lean back against the thwart and wonder how I'm going to keep going, or find the breath to speak.

"A place... pointed out to me... don't know...can spot it," I gasp.

"Give it your best shot," Max says. He seems to be having a hell of a time. "The sooner we find it the better. It gets dark early in these canyons."

* * *

I nearly miss it. My attention strays to the splash of green caught in the limb of a half submerged tree on the right. My little friend with the Taser. I swallow and look back to my left just in time to spot what I hope is the exit point.

"Over there, Max, where that little eddy is."

Max spots the place and works the canoe over to it. A large boulder creates the back current that allows us to hold our place while we examine the rock.

"Not bad," Max announces.

I look from the rock wall to Max and then back to the wall. It looks steep and difficult to me. "You're kidding, right?"

"Pull yourself up on that little shelf there. I'm afraid we're going to have to let the shotgun go with the canoe. Not enough hands to go around."

"We're letting the canoe go? Can't we tie it off? What if we can't make it up this thing?"

"Can't leave it here. Might as well have a billboard saying 'here we are'."

I put a hand on the rock shelf. The shale slab sticks out about a foot and a half and is about six feet long, maybe two feet above the water line. I steady the canoe as much as I can, then slowly shift my weight until I have two hands flat on the shale. Holding the canoe tight with my legs I slowly raise my body. Finally, I'm sitting on the shelf. In the blink of an eye Max is standing on the shelf next to me. The canoe is already starting to drift away.

"Max, I'm not sure our situation has improved any."

"Don't worry, John. This thing is like a highway. Just follow me and do what I do. If you need a hand up, say so. Now come on, let's get this done, rain clouds coming in."

He reaches over his head and grabs a handhold, plants one foot on the rock and swings up until the other foot sits on a protrusion. He does the same thing again and is standing twelve feet over my head looking down at me.

I try to ignore my shaking knees and my sweaty palms. I reach up to the handhold Max used. I'm able to get a pretty good grip, which surprises me. I bring my knee up to my chest and plant my sneaker against the rock and push away. My other hand joins my first and I find a place about four feet up where I can plant my foot. I quickly move one hand to a new hold about eye level. I'm conscious of the water rushing by below me, but I'm starting to believe this can work.

In fact, after the next round of push off and grab the terrain starts to slope toward the rim.

"Take it easy now," Max calls. "It looks easier, but if you don't take your time you'll start to slide back, then you're done. Take your time."

I do. In all it's probably thirty feet to the top, the terrain a dark brown mud with shale and scrub brush, redolent with the smell of dank earth. My feet want to slip a few inches in the damp earth with each step, and I dig my fingers into the earth around each handhold. We make it just as the heavy drops begin to fall. My hands and forearms are cramping.

"You were holding on much harder than you had to," Max says. "Common error when you start out." Max, on the other hand, seems to be fresh as a daisy. "Let's get some cover, find a secure spot for the night."

"For the night?" It's almost dusk, and I thought we'd find a road and get out of here.

"The map I looked at shows there's not much on this side for several miles. If anyone is looking for us they'll know that, too. Wouldn't be hard to set up and wait for us. There are only one or two exit points."

We enter the pine forest and find a spot Max is happy with. From under the boughs of the pine he has a good view of the area, and it backs up against a rock outcropping, giving us cover to the rear. We sit with our backs to the trunk. The branches keep the rain, which has gotten heavier, off us. There is pinesap however.

"This is gonna ruin my t-shirt, Max."

Max grins, like there's no place he'd rather be. "Maybe Willie will send you another one."

"You really think those guys are still out there?"

"Good chance. There were sent to do a job. Granted, they were careless, and they paid for it. They never should have approached the camp in that formation, especially after seeing that there were three vehicles there. Although I bet they knew who one of them belonged to."

"You think they knew?"

"They were a cleanup crew. Didn't expect any problems. They

were sloppy, and now they're embarrassed. I bet they're well trained. Their leader let them down. They won't make any more mistakes. All we can hope, really, is that they report their status and get called back to base."

"And who's at base, Max? Who's behind this?"

"Whoever paid to kill Kenneth Dixon," he looks over at me. "For some reason they figure they have to kill you, too."

41

Warehouse Row, New York Area

Boris is at the warehouse early the next morning when the truck returns. The hidden rear doors swing open and the SUV is on the ground in minutes. Boris and Victor watch as the body of the dead commando is taken into the ready room. The leader of the group approaches Boris to make his report.

"Well," Boris demands.

"We searched both sides of the river, but there was no sign of them. We covered the exit areas, but, again, no contact." The man stands ramrod straight as he gives his report, staring ahead, unblinking. "We recovered the canoe downriver, empty. From the cliffs we sighted a body caught in some driftwood. Pavel. The heavy rains carried the body downriver before we could recover it."

"Is there any way you could have fucked this assignment up more," Boris says through clenched teeth. The ex-soldier shows no reaction. "See if you can get rid of the body without screwing that up, too."

The man takes a step back, does an about face and goes into the ready room.

Victor watches his boss, his own eyes as blank as the ex-soldiers. He waits. He doesn't have to wait long.

"We have to step away from Mann just now. Too many questions will be asked. He might have government protection. Have you kept track of his sister, like I asked?"

"Yes, she's in France taking photo's in a cave. There are about twenty involved, but she has decided to work late a few times. Her driver is keeping an eye on her for us."

Boris nods his head. "Have our friends in Marseilles kidnap her.

No harm, in case there has to be some contact. Ideally there won't. Mann will just know that his beloved sister has disappeared. It shouldn't take him long to figure out what he has to do to get her back. Once Broner is acquitted and dead, we'll teach Mr. Mann a lesson."

42

FBI Office, Albany, New York

"Hello, Agent Greene. Trooper Tim Murphy here. Talked to Detective Callahan, he told me you had the Dixon case now."

Greene cradled the phone and reached for his pen and a legal pad. "That's right. Something up?"

"Well, I was in Albany the day Dixon was killed, for a meeting. I was heading out when the call came in. I spotted Broner and picked him up."

"Good job, fast work."

"Thanks. My area is up in the mountains and the detectives told me that Mann had a place up here and to let them know if anything out of the ordinary went on."

"Has it?"

"I've got a banged up canoe on shore at the river access. Ran the registration and it's Mann's. I've also got a corpse, looks like a drowning, found by some fisherman under a bridge down stream."

Greene really didn't like where this was going. "Is it Mann?" He held his breath.

"No, I've seen Mann. This was a smaller guy, dressed like a tourist, except for no ID."

"Could you go check on Mann for me?"

"I'm in my cruiser now, headed that way. Its on the other side of the river...Hold on."

"What?"

"Two guys just stepped out of the woods, flagging me down. One of 'em is Mann."

"You sure?"

"Oh yeah. Still got the Willie Nelson shirt on."

43

Law Offices, Manhattan

Eli Massry was sitting at his desk with his fists balled and the look of a madman on his face. Most astonishing was that he made no attempt to disguise his fury. A tall woman in a navy blue suit, dark hair cut short, severe glasses countering a pretty face, knocked once and entered the spacious office.

"Father, what's wrong?" Idel was Massry's only child. She'd followed her father into the legal profession and now worked in the office beside him. He would proudly admit to his friends that she was sharper than he was. No mean feat.

"The so-called Justice Department."

"The Broner case? I thought you had some pretty good leads to trade."

"So did I, dear, so did I."

"What happened?"

"Broner got involved with a very big fish when he took the job to kill Dixon. The tie in should open all this man's dealings up to the type of inspection that could blow the *mafiya* wide open, shut down a huge money laundering operation, the whole works. It should cripple their illegal operations and probably send a good few of them into a federal pen for a very long time. This was a golden opportunity for us. To eradicate this man and the scum he represents."

The young woman took the chair on the other side of the desk facing him.

"What happened?"

"The Federal Prosecutor has so much as told me that this man, Boris Sarnow, is off limits. That the testimony Broner gives isn't strong enough to change that."

"How can that be? Even a cursory investigation should provide sufficient evidence for an indictment. They're the Justice Department."

"The Feds have gone after him before, and got beat up badly in the process. The big money interests, the corporations, the Russian Embassy, have all unified to deflect the efforts made to investigate him and his minions. That was before Enron, and the black eye Justice got for strong-arming employers to cut their executives loose, and to not pay their attorney's bills. No, he assured me, they won't be going after Boris Sarnow any time soon, and certainly not based on the information Jason Broner is willing to trade."

"If the Government won't go after him, who will?"

The old warrior looked at his daughter, shaking his head. "I have a commitment to this client, but in reality I only took him on to get to the people that hired him. God help me, but I care more about taking Boris Sarnow down than getting Broner off. I still feel sure that whatever gave rise to the need to kill Kenneth Dixon could bring down the house of cards Sarnow has been so carefully constructing since he came to America."

"Will Justice do anything?"

"No. They don't intend to even perform a follow up investigation. No one will meet with Sarnow and question him about Kenneth Dixon. No subpoena will be issued, no Court Order to produce records, calendars, e-mails. Through the legitimate cover he's created Boris has been able to blind them to the illegal side of things."

"Is there anything we can do, Father?"

Massry swings his chair toward the window. He sets his jaw. "Somehow we'll have to obtain enough evidence to make them pay attention. We'll have to do this without the benefit of police, prosecutors, or courts."

Idel nods her head slowly in agreement. "Once again, the righteous are left to their own methods while the law and the government protect the rich, wicked and the unlawful."

44

Prehistoric Caves, Southern France

"Mark, I'll be done in about twenty minutes. You can start taking some of this excess stuff out to the car, if you want."

Yvette is pleased with the progress she's made. Her part of the project is wrapped up. She's also pleased that they had told Alain they wouldn't need his services today. Mark had an old beat up Honda civic, and it was doing just fine. Dr. Sullivan appeared perplexed by the request, but agreed, and provided a stipend to Mark for the use of his car. Sullivan also invited her to stay on for a few more days, if she wanted. After all, the rooms at the hotel were rented as a block. She told him she would think about it.

After about ten minutes Yvette realizes that Mark has made a couple of trips to the car, but seems to be gone for a while now. She hopes he hasn't fallen or tripped on something. Or hit his head again. The team tried to make the cave as safe as possible, but it was still a cave. She works her way along the reflected path, the LED's popping on as she approaches and going off as she moves past them. After a few minutes she's at the entrance to the large cavern that marks the beginning of the cave network. What she sees stops her dead in her tracks.

Entering the cavern from the side opposite is a roughly dressed man. In one large hand he holds a pistol. His other hand is holding a very pale and terrified intern by the arm. The pistol is pointed at Mark's head.

45

Adirondack Mountains

"Here we are," I call out from the back seat as Murphy pulls to the side of the road and motions the rest of our cavalcade down the gravel and dirt road that leads to the camp.

There's a SWAT truck and a crime scene van.

"They're going to make sure the black SUV crowd are gone, and secure the site," Murphy explains. Max and trooper Tim Murphy sit in front. Rank has privilege, as they say. Seems the trooper served two tours in Afghanistan with a Ranger unit. He and Max have worked some of the same neighborhoods. Murphy's radio spits into life.

"OK to proceed, watch the taped areas."

Murphy acknowledges and we ease onto the track and slowly head toward the cabin.

"That must be the Taser guy's rental," Max says as we slowly pass by.

"It'll get a good once over by the crime scene crowd," Murphy assures him.

We get out and make our way up to the cabin, careful to respect the boundaries set up. As we get close I can see the cabin is riddled with bullet holes. The remains of the C-2 are still on the table where we left it. Crime scene people are staking out a dark patch in the dirt.

Murphy shakes his head and whistles. "Nice shot. That guy bled out while his buddies were chasing you? Mercenaries?"

Max just nods, not surprised. "Eastern European, Russian, maybe Chechen. They probably had it easy for too long, discipline got lax. They'll have a score to settle, if they're given the chance."

Murphy puts his hands on his hips, looks at Max.

119

"I keep some pretty heavy firepower in my trunk. Keep me in the loop, OK?"

Max smiles his appreciation, glances at the blood congealed in the dirt, the flies in a feeding frenzy.

"This is all because you saw someone kill Kenneth Dixon?" the trooper asks me, perplexed.

"I don't really know. None of it makes any sense to me. It sure is getting old, though."

46

Albany County Jail

Eli Massry presents himself at the Albany County Jail and endures the routine that is all too familiar, now. As he's led to the interview room he can't help but wonder how Broner will take the news he has for him. Massry doesn't like Broner, normally would be happy to prosecute him himself. But Broner has something on Boris Sarnow, who is proving to be untouchable.

The key turns and the door swings open to reveal Jason Broner, head raised, arrogant hope in his eyes. Massry's stern look isn't promising.

"I've spoken with the government's attorneys. They're the ones who would go after Sarnow, who would recommend you for witness protection," he pauses, making sure the man before him understands his plight. "They don't believe that your evidence is credible or strong enough to justify their involvement." Massry watches as Broner's bravado crumbles.

"I've played my last card. They're gonna kill me." The fright shows in his eyes as he stares at Massry. His wild eyes roam around the small room until they finally light on his clenched and cuffed hands. "Oh, shit!" he wails.

"We have to get more," Massry says calmly, the tone reasonable.

Broner looks up at him, head in hands, but unseeing. He stays like that for some time.

"More?" Broner finally croaks. Massry nods his head in assent.

"What does that mean?" his eyes show no comprehension, only the panicked frenzy of the trapped animal.

"We have to get more solid evidence of Boris Sarnow's

involvement than we have now. We have to be able to make a case the authorities can't ignore."

"How?" the same eyes look back at Massry, unbelieving.

"We'll have to work on that. Start by going over everything again, see if there's something you left out that might be important. We'll have to follow leads that otherwise the police would be investigating." Massry spreads his hands on the metal tabletop. "We might have to hire investigators. Perhaps we can put your friend the tail back to work. At the least, I need to talk to him, find out if he has more that could help us. We need more. We need to be able to make the case, and it has to be strong enough that they can't ignore it. The Justice Department will want to get this guy if we can give them enough, but they aren't going to sacrifice themselves in the process." Massry leans forward, he has Broner's attention. "You told me that if you go inside, into the general prison population, they'll have you killed the first day." Massry lets this sink in, then takes out his legal pad. "Let's start again, from the beginning. It's you or them."

Broner nods his agreement, shows some animation, even if still struggling through a heavy fog.

47

FBI Office, Albany, New York

Greene is staring out his window. He's oblivious to the early autumn colors. The natural beauty of the landscape was far from his thoughts. James Ostermann, the US Attorney for the Northern District of New York, a man Greene has always respected, has just told Greene something that runs against every fiber in his being.

"I'm sorry, John, but the people that back this guy are so big it's scary. It's not just the politicians, they're just fronting for the money this guy represents. That money is huge, old, and it's everywhere. And that money is rabid. Anybody goes near this guy, their career is over. Period."

The conversation was short. Not bad enough, his PA has just let him know he has a visitor.

"Please send Mr. Bobo in," he tells his PA.

Max, with his silver crew cut, creased khaki pants and blue dress shirt is all business as he walks in and sticks out his hand. Greene can hear that his own voice is strained as he greets Max, asks him to take a seat. "What can we do for you, Max?"

"Been a little busy with John Mann. I'm sure you've heard. Greene, this is bigger than anybody thought. This wasn't some penny ante grudge killing. Dixon was on to something. We've got to find out what. Where's your investigation at?"

Just the words Greene was hoping not to hear. "We have no investigation, Max. Justice has told us to stand down."

"Fuckin' hell, Greene," he says as his jaw clenches and he glances out the window. He looks back at Greene. "They're that big?"

"I can't say anymore, Max. They won't even identify them to me.

Probably shouldn't have said what I did." Greene loses it, shouts, "but I'm pissed off Max, OK?"

Max sits with his lips pursed, while both men, red faced, look anyplace but at each other. A moment passes. "You're one of the good guys, John. I've always known that. I also know what these bastards are like. That's why I go off the reservation every once in a while. We're gonna do what's right here, John, in spite of those cowards who can't look past their own wallets. If I need you, John, I'm gonna make that call. I'll try not to ask for something that'll cost you your job or your pension, but if I need you, John, I really need you. Got it?"

Greene looks up. He nods his assent.

A moment passes before Max says, "Have you got anything for me?"

Greene blinks and takes a breath.

"Broner's got new counsel. Ely Massry. The best out there. Pro Bono. He wants these guys as much as you and I do, Max. He'll fight this all the way if he can find a way to do it."

"Maybe I should talk to this guy. Will he talk to the witness's uncle-in-law, or whatever the fuck I am?"

"From what I know, Max, he won't just pass the ammunition, he'll load the guns."

48

Pre-historic Cave, Southern France

"Get your hands off him," she shouts. "You want to steal stuff, go ahead. There's not much here. Leave him alone."

Yvette marches out into the main cavern, past the equipment bags and crates, to confront the large scruffy man holding Mark. Her eyes blaze as she sees Alain walk through the cavern opening behind him. Mark is then passed to Alain.

"Very nice," says the man with the pistol, as his eyes undress Yvette. "Is this her?" he asks Alain.

"That's the one," Alain says with a nod of his head.

"You're coming with me," says the man with the pistol, and grabs for her arm.

Yvette deftly pulls away, at the same time sending a kick into his balls worthy of Ronan O'Gara. The man's eyes roll into his head as he drops his gun and doubles over. Alain moves to pick up the gun. Yvette kicks it away and grabs Mark, pushing him towards the passageway she just came through.

As they run back into the passageway Yvette finds that she's being slowed by darkness. They're outpacing the motion sensors on the LEDs, which are coming on after they've run by. Still they try to go faster until Yvette bangs her head on one of the overhangs and falls to the ground. Mark kneels at her side and shakes her shoulder.

"Yvette, are you OK? Yvette, come on."

She touches her head as she sits up, her hand comes away sticky. She looks at it in the dim light of the lamp, sees blood. She shakes her head to clear it and they continue.

"Yvette, we're going to have to slow down, or we'll bang our heads again."

"I think I have a plan, Mark. See if these lights have a turn-off switch."

Mark quickly picks one up and examines it.

"Here, on the back," he whispers.

"Mark, turn off every other one, that'll slow him down if he follows us."

"He'll follow us," Mark says. "I heard him telling Alain that he was to kidnap you."

Yvette stares at Mark's grim face, which disappears as he turns the light he's holding off. The darkness crowds in, bringing with it the damp smells of rock and dirt. She's immediately disoriented. She'll have to move along the passageway to activate the next light, but isn't sure which direction to go in. She could easily walk into the cave wall. Mark turns the light back on, his eyes wide with the same fear she feels. She takes a deep breath and moves along until the next light comes on and Mark joins her. They leapfrog along that way, turning every other motion sensor and light off. A passage comes in from the left.

"Mark, watch your head here, the ground slopes up, not really a problem going in, but a big problem coming out if you're not careful."

They enter the passage and kneel down by a variety of equipment.

"Let's hope Dr. Sullivan left the sound equipment set up."

It is. Yvette finds the wire that allows remote activation. She carefully feeds it back to the main tunnel and around the corner to where she had been working earlier. The space is a bit wider. She crouches against the wall.

"Mark, turn off the lights here. Leave them on in the passage. And bring that strobe and battery pack into the other tunnel, put it where the sound gear is."

The silence is heavy, broken only by the sound of their feet shuffling. What seems like an eternity is in fact only a few minutes. They adjust the motion-activated lights to lead their pursuer into the side tunnel and hide themselves around the corner in the dark. They have the remotes for both the strobe and the sound. Yvette takes a kerchief from around her neck and holds it to her head. The bleeding seems to have stopped. They wait in the dark, conscious of their own heavy breathing.

With only every other light coming on he moves slowly, his heavy boots kicking the breakdown rock that litters the tunnel floor. He's being mindful of the uneven ceiling. They can track his progress from the reflection of the LEDs on the far tunnel wall, more light as he gets closer. They make themselves as small as possible, hug the darkness. They can see his shadow. He's almost past the critical passage when one of the LEDs down that tunnel lights up. He pauses, peers in, and then slowly moves up the small incline and into the tunnel.

"Here goes," she whispers. "Close your eyes."

With a remote in each hand she presses her thumbs down. The world explodes. Everything happens at once. The strobe gives a half second blinding flash at the same time the sound blast hits, and a dozen screaming wild boar come racing down the tunnel, or so it seems. The kidnapper can't help himself. He drops the gun and turns to flee, dashing to escape. From where they are around the corner, even with the echoes reverberating through the passages, they hear the sickening crunch as the 'kidnapper' runs face first into the overhang.

Mark quickly gets the lights back on as Yvette inspects their catch. He's out cold. Blood pours out of a gash in his forehead and from his broken nose. She sees a brown stained tooth lying on the ground next to him. They roll him over with some difficulty. He's a big man.

Using the wires from the remotes they bind his hands behind him, then his ankles. They tie his feet and hands together. Hogtying him somehow seems appropriate. Yvette retrieves the pistol and she and Mark sit down with their backs against the tunnel wall, out of breath.

"I think he'll be all right if we leave him here like this. I don't think he'll bleed to death, do you?" Yvette looks over at Mark.

"Fuck him," he says.

Yvette hefts the pistol, examines it. "Let's go see how our friend Alain is getting on."

49

Montreal, Canada

Robert notices a slight shake in his voice as he answers the telephone. "Yes?"

"This is Inspector David Hanley with the RCMP. We're investigating an incident that occurred on the St. Lawrence River." The man has a calm voice. His tone says this is just routine, sorry to bother you. "Records at the marina indicate that you were on the river during the time we're interested in."

"I see," he says, as calm as he can manage.

"I'd like to stop by and talk to you about anything you might have seen or heard that might be of help to us."

Robert swallows twice. "Certainly."

"I can be there in half an hour, if that's convenient?"

"That will be fine" Robert says.

The inspector ends the call.

"Well?" Jurga asks from behind him. He turns and looks at her. She's been drying the dinner dishes, and now the dishrag is wound tightly between her clenched hands. The gleaming appliances and bright colors can't offset the darkness in her mind. Her wide eyes mirror the fear he feels.

"The RCMP is investigating an 'incident' on the St. Lawrence. The records show we were there." His voice is flat.

Jurga sobs, turns into the sitting room and throws herself on the sofa. Robert goes to sit with her and gently puts his hand on her shoulder.

"We have no other hope," he says. Jurga turns and buries her face in his chest.

"I know," she says.

They sit and hold each other, twenty minutes that seem like an eternity, until the two tones from the front doorbell break the spell. Robert rises and answers it, while Jurga quickly dries her eyes. Robert returns shortly with a plain-clothes officer of middle age with sharp features and a kind face. He shows them his credentials.

"Can I get you some tea or coffee, maybe a glass of water," asks Jurga.

"No, thanks very much," says Inspector Hanley as he settles on the edge of a stuffed armchair. His smile is comforting, his manner helpful. He takes a small notebook and a pen from the inside pocket of his jacket. He looks at them expectantly, but they remain mute.

"As I mentioned, the records at the marina show that you had a rental for two days," he gives them the dates. "Is that right?" They both nod yes. "I suppose you wouldn't be going upriver, it gets pretty rough when you get any closer to Lake Ontario." They nod again. He seems to look at them for a beat longer than necessary, then consults his notes. The silence is maddening for Robert and Jurga, but they don't say anything, they're struck dumb. Hanley knows what he's doing, and notes their discomfort.

"There was a terrible incident at one of the Islands. A houseboat, the same type that you had rented, was destroyed by a blast of some sort. Six young men were on board, and died as a result of the explosion." He stops and looks from Robert to Jurga, an enquiring expression on his face. They simply stare back.

"Did you see this other boat at all in your travels?"

Robert clears his throat. "We did see a boat like ours moored at one of the docks. We went to another island as a result, further upriver. In the morning we headed back to the marina."

Hanley nods his head. "Did you see any other boats in the vicinity, or anything suspicious?"

"There was another boat at the same dock, like a speedboat. It didn't look like it was there for the night, though."

Hanley nods again, folds his notebook and sits back in the chair. His eyes move from Robert to Jurga and back to Robert.

"You see," he says, "the thing is, this explosion doesn't appear to have been an accident. Our crime scene people tell us that their investigation of the wreckage shows that a bomb of some type was planted on the boat. Nothing in our investigation, so far, shows any motive for someone to kill any of the six men that were on board that boat." He lets this sink in, and continues. "It occurred to us that perhaps there was a case of mistaken identity involved. Please forgive this question, but we have to follow every lead in a tragic situation like this. Is there anyone that would have a reason to kill you?"

The question hangs in the air like a scimitar about to drop. Hands held, white knuckled, Robert and Jurga answer with one voice. "Yes." After a moments silence, a squeeze from Robert and a look from Hanley, Jurga breaks down.

"When we got home there was a message from my brother," she sobs. "My parents were executed by a sniper while tilling their garden, just as the pictures showed." She puts her head on Robert's shoulder and he holds her close.

"My widowed mother was found tortured, raped, and murdered." His voice catches in his throat, "How can these animals be stopped?"

"Do you have any idea who might have done these things? And why?"

Robert clears his throat.

"We received photos, which we took to be a threat, what would happen to our parents if we refused to do something."

"Refused to do what?" asks Hanley.

"We didn't know at first," Robert says. "Then we got instructions. A suitcase. Aluminum. It was placed in our garage. We were told how to proceed."

Hanley is starting to look very uncomfortable.

"How were you told to proceed?"

"We brought it to an island. Hid it. We were told to stay overnight nearbye. We did. We heard an explosion and saw the remains in the morning," Jurga sobs.

Hanley slowly shakes his head, mind racing.

"Look, you've been through a lot. On your own. Thank you for being truthfull with me. We're going to help you now. This event could have international ramifications. I'd like you to come to the station with me. I'll need to get your statement in writing, and I'll need to involve our national security people."

"What will happen then?" Jurga asks, tearful. "What will become of us?"

Hanson looks at them for a moment, face masking his thoughts. Finally he says in a sad voice, "I don't know." He pulls out his cell phone and calls his dispatcher. "Connect me to the Commissioner's office. It's urgent."

50

Manhattan

Security seems very good at the Upper East Side apartment building where Eli Massry lives. Max called him late the previous day. Massry didn't sound enthusiastic, but he let Max explain his proposition. More importantly, he agreed to meet. Max caught the early train and then took a cab from Penn Station to Massry's front door. The attendant cum security guard at the front desk sat behind a thick glass window.

"I have an appointment with Mr. Massry," Max tells the guy, who looks him up and down, deciding if he'll let him pass.

"Please put any metal you're carrying in the tray and push it through. Then go through the detector."

Max isn't surprised at the security in the place. The guard nearly falls over as Max pulls his Berretta from the holster at the small of his back and places it in the tray.

"You have to have a New York City license to carry that here," the guard says in a raised voice.

"I do," he says simply, finishing with his phone, belt, and spare change.

The guard phones for clearance, then OK's the elevator doors to open, and presets the floor it's going to.

Max relaxes to some classical music as he's transported to one of the penthouse units. A fellow a lot larger than Max waits as the elevator door opens, gives him a long look, a frisking, and an invitation to wait in the next room. The room offers a panoramic view of the New York skyline. Within a minute a door opens to the side and Massry walks in. He's not a large man, but he radiates a certain confidence, an assurance that wouldn't be taken for granted. He looks intently at Max, who calmly returns his stare.

"Thanks for seeing me."

Massry nods. He gestures to a pair of comfortable looking leather chairs arranged by the window near a table with an oriental lamp on it. They sit and face each other.

Massry offers refreshment, Max refuses. "Let's get to it then," Massry says.

"My friend saw your client kill a man," Max begins. Massry is impassive, listening. "Since then four men have died trying to kill my friend. It occurs to me that they believe that without my friend's testimony your client gets off." Max leans forward in his chair. "We don't believe that your client has that kind of muscle. We think he was hired. By some very connected people. We think that Kenneth Dixon was killed because of something he was working on. We also believe that the people behind Dixon's murder will eventually kill my friend. That's the way they work."

Massry blinks, but doesn't change expression, as if telling Max to continue.

"The authorities seem to be ignoring information you've given them about who your client worked for. We need to know what that info is. We think the authorities might be afraid to go after the people behind this without an airtight case. If we can, we'll give them one. That way my friend gets free of this."

Max sits and watches Massry.

"I think the law enforcement agencies are capable of following up on any leads they've come up with," Massry says without emotion.

Max smiles. "I think you know better. I think you know that law enforcement is fighting a losing battle here. They're hands are tied too much of the time. Lawyers, don't take offense, tell them what they can do, what they can't. That's not the way crimes get solved. That's the way investigators get tired and frustrated, and retire early. We don't have those limitations. We don't have to follow the law to find our way to the people responsible." Max keeps his eyes on the other man.

"Let's say that despite all the odds you are successful at identifying someone who you are convinced is responsible. What happens then? You can't arrest them. You have to involve the same people who've already said that they're not interested in this matter. What then?" Massry asks, raising his eyebrows.

"I've been in law enforcement, I know how it works. We'd like to get enough information, proof if you will, to convince the police and the prosecutors to do their job and put those responsible where they belong. That might be enough, combined with what your man might know, to do the job."

Massry purses his lips. "I know of you, Mr. Bobo. You have quite a strong reputation in law enforcement circles. Although the record isn't public, your reputation outside of the legal system is probably stronger."

Max doesn't change expression. "As I say, we'd like to find the proof. As I think you suggest, there are other ways of removing the problem."

Massry slowly shakes his head up and down, a slight frown on his pale face, dark features hiding whatever thoughts he might have.

"What do you think I can do for you?"

Max nods, as if they just reached an agreement. "It doesn't add up that your guy was robbing Kenneth Dixon. Not his kind of work. If you figure he was hired to kill Dixon, things do start to add up. The only reason to try to kill my friend is because he's the witness that puts your client away. The people that hired Broner apparently think he knows more than they thought, more than they can chance. They want to get rid of the witness, get Broner off, and then get rid of him. They know he'll try to trade whatever he has for whatever he can get. They don't want that. Maybe I should say they didn't want that. I think Justice has sent a message that whatever Broner had wasn't enough. Not enough in their league anyway. If you tell me what Broner knows, then I know who had Ken Dixon killed, and I can find out why."

Massry nods his head. "What makes you think that you and your friends are any match for these people, in their 'league' as you say?"

"You know some things about me," Max says. "I've fought in wars, been undercover, gone 'black'. Hunted, been hunted, been an assassin. I've got contacts. I've made friends along the way. Real assets. What makes the 'league' these people play in so intimidating is that they're so ruthless. It's not that they're smart, it's mostly just that they clean up after themselves. They don't take chances. They keep their own secrets. Simply put, they're not that special, not to someone like me."

Massry frowns. "Information is all you're looking for?"

"Whatever you can do to help," Max responds.

"I'm scheduled to meet with my client later today. Can I contact you this evening?"

"I'll look forward to your call." They stand and shake hands, not like strangers.

51

Southern France

They stumble into the lobby of the hotel. Fortunately, it's the closest place to the roads leading from the cave.

"Yvette, what's happened? You're bleeding. Mark, what's going on?"

Dr. James Sullivan was heading back to his room after enjoying the cuisine in the hotel's luxurious dining room when he spotted Yvette and Mark enter the lobby.

"You won't believe it, Doc. Yvette was almost kidnapped. You showed them, though, didn't you, Yvette?"

Mark is literally bouncing around, the post trauma adrenalin rush almost more than he can handle.

"Is that true?" the director can't hide his astonishment. "Come over here and sit down. What happened to your head?" He leads her to one of the fancy banquettes that line the walls. Some potted plants provide a modicum of privacy.

Yvette sits down, realizes her hands are shaking.

"We were finished and started to clean up," she began.

"I got grabbed taking stuff to the car," Mark said.

"There was a real rough looking guy holding him when I got to the main cave. Then Alain came in."

Sullivan's face hardens as he hears of Alain's involvement.

"Yvette told them to take what they wanted, but leave me alone," Mark adds, still pumped.

"We got away into the tunnel. I hit my head on an overhang."

"How did you get away," Sullivan says.

"We tricked the kidnapper. Got him in the side tunnel, the one with the boars?"

"No," Sullivan's eyes go wide.

"Yep. Hit him with the strobe and the herd at the same time. He ran himself into the rock overhang. Out cold."

"We tied him up and Yvette took his gun," Mark adds. "You should've seen that Alain's face. He's leaning against the van smoking when he hears us and turns around. Yvette sticks the gun in his face. His mouth dropped open and the cigarette fell out. Burned his shirt." Mark can't stop grinning.

"And then we drove here. It's the closest place where we knew we'd be safe."

"Hmm... I hope you're right." Sullivan has had experience working in dangerous places and learned long ago to take nothing for granted. "So those two are trussed up at the cave," he says, almost to himself. "OK. First, Yvette, you're going to the hospital. We can't take a chance on any brain swelling. It can take hours to happen, but then it's too late. Meantime, I'll have one of the other staff pack your bag and collect your gear. You're going home on the first flight out."

"Jim, I'm sure its nothing. It's over, now."

"No. If you weren't so brave you'd be kidnapped, both of you. Then what?" He takes her hand and rubs it between both of his. "No. We'll take no chances. Meanwhile, I'll get the gendarmes on the case, try and find out what's going on here. Get some answers. What's the reason. Are we in danger? Should we halt the project?"

"Oh, Jim. I'm so sorry."

"You have nothing to be sorry for. That bastard Alain does, though. OK, let's get moving. I want you checked out and safe, ASAP." Sullivan looks over at Mark. "How about you, young man? Any wounds to report?"

52

Albany County Jail

Massry notices the strange attack on the senses that accompanies his visits to Broner. Overpowering smells. Body odor and antiseptic, a strange and primitive bazaar. Then there are the sounds. No acoustic relief. The jarring sounds of metal on metal, the slap of leather on cement. Eerie echoes, unintelligible except as anger, fear, or frustration. Drab colors, a socialist planet controlled by bureaucrats.

They come to the interview room, the guard unlocks the door and Massry enters. Broner sits the same way as when Massry first met him, but he's changed. Not a tough guy with a hole card anymore, or with a method that keeps him from getting caught. Massry sits down, folds his hands, and looks at Broner.

"I have been contacted by people who want your help in finding those who hired you." Broner doesn't respond. "They want to free the witness from the threat of retaliation, they want to see justice meted out to the people who ordered Kenneth Dixon's death, and they want to know why Dixon's death was necessary."

Broner slowly lifts his head and looks into Massry's face.

"It seems they have already been successful in preventing three attempts to kill the witness. For some reason they have been unusually effective against these people. If they are somehow successful in attaining their goals you benefit in several ways. One, the Government might receive a case they can't turn away from, a solid case. That would make your testimony more important to the authorities and at the same time make you less of a threat to those who would have you killed.

"Two, I have been led to believe that if they can't get satisfaction through legal means, they are prepared to remove the threat by illegal means. Permanent means. That would remove the threat to you by removing the person making the threat. Not a total solution for you, but a great improvement over where you are now."

Massry pauses. Broner's eyes meet Massry's, comprehension slow to take hold. He blinks once, twice. His mouth opens. His mouth closes.

"What do they want from me?"

"Whatever you can give them to help them find the source of all this."

"Like what?"

"Essentially what you've told me, the cooperation of the fellow you used as your 'tail' could be very helpful to them. They have a sense of what they're after, but they don't have a name."

"What do I have to do?"

"You either authorize me to provide information, to cooperate, or you arrange a visitation with them and tell them your story."

Broner rubs his bristled chin and narrows his eyes. He appears to have trouble comprehending. He looks at Massry. "You tell them, tell them everything. Anything they want, anything at all. Tell Jonny to help them. Please, please, have them hurry."

53

FBI, Albany, New York

Greene rubs his eyes and realizes how tired he is. Another terror threat coming in from Canada. This one across the St. Lawrence. A light aluminum suitcase. Homeland says it's too light to be nuclear. What else? What now? Best guess, some kind of attack is imminent. His phone buzzes.

"Agent Greene, it's John Mann."

"Oh, hi, Mr. Mann. How're you doing after your ordeal at the camp?" Greene swivels his chair to the window.

"They tried to kidnap Yvette."

Greene snaps upright. "I thought she was in France?"

"That's where it happened, at the cave shoot."

"Is she all right?"

"She got away, a bump on her head, but nothing serious. She's on her way home."

"Is Max still with you?"

"He is now, but he's doing some travel to unearth whatever he can about the people behind this. He'll be here until she gets in, though."

"I'd like to debrief her, then see what kind of protective cover we can arrange for when Max is away."

"Thanks, Agent Greene. I'll give you a call."

"OK, Mr. Mann. Stay safe."

54

Manhattan, Boris' HQ

Boris has a bemused smile still on his face as he leaves Svetlana in the private apartment in their Manhattan office complex. He enters his office in a good mood. Everything is in place. He leaves for Memphis in a couple of days. He cradles the phone on his shoulder and leans back. He holds a pencil between his fingers.

"Hello, Victor. What is it?"

"Three things. First, the girl, Mann's sister. She escaped from the men sent to abduct her. We can't locate her, but she's probably on her way back to New York."

"What about the agents we used?"

"They were tied up and left in the cave. One nearly died of a head injury. He's in hospital, but both are under custody of the gendarmerie."

"What else?"

"Mann seems to be in some loose form of protective custody. Some type of former government agent is staying close to him."

"OK. What else?"

"Broner has a new lawyer representing him," the voice from Albany sounds as if it's in the next room.

"Who?"

"Eli Massry."

Snap! The two pencil halves bounce off the wall.

55

JFK

We meet the Air France Jetliner at JFK. We drive down in one of those big Chevy utility vehicles with blacked out windows. On the way we stop and pick up an associate of Max's named Reid. No first name necessary, it seems. Reid is about my age, forties. He exudes the same quiet confidence and competence that Max does, I assume for the same reason. Reid is fit and alert and on the job. He stays parked outside the terminal as Max and I go in to meet Yvette.

I spot her as soon as she comes out of the customs exit. She's pushing a trolley piled high with suitcases and gear. There's a bandage wrapped around her head, but she looks great. She spots me and runs over. We embrace. She sees Max.

"What's that asshole doing here?"

I remember the last time she saw him was at Jenny's and Susan's funeral, not one of his finest moments, as he's admitted to me. I also realize I haven't filled her in on all that's happened since she was in France. The NASCAR guy with the taser, the commando assassins, Max showing up and saving me. The river.

"Glad you're in good form, Yvette," Max says. "Long time no see." He sticks out his hand to shake. "I was way out of line last time we saw each other. I'm sorry, I'm trying to make up for it."

She glares at him, looks at his hand like she might bite it, then looks at me. I smile and shake my head in a 'it's alright' kind of way. Her jawline hardens, but she shakes his hand. She looks back at me.

"You got some splainin' to do."

As we exit the terminal I see Reid standing at the Chevy scanning the area. Max is doing the same. This isn't lost on Yvette, and she gives me a questioning look. Once we're in the back seat Reid loads the luggage into the car while Max keeps up the surveillance. After a brief introduction Reid heads out, Max settled in the front seat, listening to everything that's said.

"Tell me about France," I say. She does. My stomach turns sour when I think of what might have happened. The fear I haven't allowed to feel for myself suddenly comes to the fore.

Yvette sees this and takes my hand. "What is it? Do you know something about this?"

"I'm afraid so," and I tell her all my misadventures since we parted in Ireland. When I finish I see that she has tears in her eyes. Her lip trembles.

Yvette reaches out and puts her hand on Max' shoulder. She gives it a warm squeeze. "Thank you."

56

North Albany, New York

Max spots the Quonset hut in the run down industrial park. He slows, coasting along beside the weeds and trash that almost cover the sidewalk. He comes to the curb cut and carefully drives over the cracked concrete and into the yard. He turns the engine off, the ticking of it cooling the only sound. It's a sunny day, and he spots the man standing in the shadowy garage opening. Max figures he's about five foot eight, thin and wiry. Dirty blue work clothes. Worrying an oil rag in his hands. Nervous. The man walks hesitantly out of the shadows and stands in the garage doorway.

"Jonny?" Max calls out, getting out of the truck. "Did Eli call you?" Act familiar with 'Eli', the guy that's Broner's savior. The little guy nods 'yes'.

Max smiles. He leans against the front of the truck, taking his time. Like a pigeon working for a nut, Jonny slowly approaches Max. Somewhere a train whistle blows. Max extends his hand when Jonny gets close enough. They shake.

"Look, Jonny," Max bends his head forward and tilts it a little to the side, sort of a 'can I be honest with you here' kind of look. "I'm not law enforcement, OK?" Jonny takes this in without reaction. "In fact, I've been known to work outside the law to do what has to get done," he says, a pause to let it sink in. "Do we understand each other here."

Jonny starts to loosen up a little, actually nods his agreement.

"Look, I know you talked to Eli, and I'm sure he told you this, but I'll say it again…to keep Jason alive we have to take down some big people."

Jonny's head is bobbing up and down now. Max pushes off the

truck, puts a hand on Jonny's shoulder and they start to walk toward the coolness of the garage.

"From what I'm told, your skills are the reason we know who ordered the trigger on Dixon." Max stops and faces him. "I've been doing undercover work it seems all my life," Max says. "I admire what you're able to do."

"Thanks," Jonny says. "I'll do whatever I can to help."

"I hope you know more by now. I need you to show me where and how they operate. We have to bring them down to get Jason out. To keep him alive. Are you in?"

Jonny's heart is beating a little fast at the flattery and the attention. But he also knows that this Max is right, he is good at this stuff. He's worked hard at it, and he was trained by some of the best. Eli Massry told Jonny who Max was. Jonny was standing before a legend.

"Show me what you do, how you do it," Max says.

Jonny leads Max to a workbench and pulls a couple of boxes from under a table.

"These are pretty simple bugs, some for listening, some record," he picks up another item and turns it so Max can see. "These track using GPS. I've worked out a lot of ways to get these on a vehicle, even if it's moving."

Max looks interested and impressed.

"Have you used this?" he says, holding the gadget in his hand.

"I bugged one of their limo's the other day just to see if it works," Jonny tells him.

"Did it?"

Jonny shakes his head yes.

"I wasn't sure at first. I had it on a filament line, and I saw it stick to the limo when it went in. But the limo never came out while I was there." He took out a roll of clear fishing line and unspun a little of it. Almost invisible. "They've got this big truck, for haulin' trash," Jonny tells him. "That's all that came out. Later when I checked the GPS on my laptop it said the limo was up at Alexandria Bay, near Canada."

"It went there after you left?" says Max.

"Couldn't. Not enough time. Only way it got there on the limo was if the limo was inside the trash hauler."

Max keeps probing and soon it's evident that Jonny could be an important asset in finding out what's been going on. He and Jonny agree to drive south to visit the warehouse the next day. Jonny has a new way of planting the GPS he wants to try out. They compare notes on appropriate 'bum' regalia. Max offers to pick Jonny up just before dawn for they're trip to the City and warehouse row. He's also going to supply the coffee and sandwiches.

Max is backing out of the yard when he looks up and sees Jonny smiling at him. Jonny waves.

Max waves back.

57

Suburbs, Albany, New York

Reid doesn't say a lot, but he's pleasant, always a half smile on his face, and he has Yvette and me feeling safe. He drives around Julia Dixon's neighborhood before driving past her house. He circles back and parks up the street for a few minutes, then drives up. I recognize Julia Dixon as soon as the door opens. Without the imposed grief of the funeral she looks beautiful.

"Please come in," she smiles as she shows Yvette and me into a comfortable sitting room. Coffee, tea, and biscuits are set out, and we help ourselves.

"Thank you for agreeing to meet with us, and on such short notice," I begin.

Julia Dixon gives a dismissive laugh. "It's me who wants to thank you. Ever since the funeral I've felt so bad about what that detective did. Agent Greene visited me and set the record straight. I've been looking for a way to apologize to you ever since. I was thrilled when you called and asked to meet."

"Agent Greene explained that they now believe someone paid to have your husband killed?" This is difficult territory and I try to be as gentle as possible.

"Yes," Julia says with a sigh, obviously distressed.

Yvette jumps in. "We believe the FBI know who the people behind it are. But without finding out why, what Ken had on them, they'll get away with it."

"You mean they know who ordered it?"

"The shooter identified who hired him. Apparently he's very high profile, and the government attorney's are afraid to go after him without a case that's bombproof."

Julia Dixon sits back. The anger in her eyes is clear. She's also curious. "Why do you care?"

Yvette answers. "They want to get their shooter off so he doesn't spill his guts to the feds. They've tried three times now to kill my brother. They tried to kidnap me while I was working in France. They won't stop unless we stop them." Julia's eyes meet Yvette's. Something passes between them.

"What can I do?" she asks.

We go over again what Ken might have been working on, how the feds went through his laptop and came up with nothing. She tells us Greene talked to Ken's boss, Bezaan, who Ken didn't care for, and came up empty.

"Was Ken acting any differently over those last weeks?" Yvette asks. "Think hard."

Julia looks at her for a moment and then says, "Yes, a little bit more tense. But one thing does stand out to me, now. He'd sometimes joke, or pun, about something he was working on. You'd know it was something only he understood."

"And he did something like that? What was it?"

Julia looks at me, then back to Yvette. "You heard the story from the funeral about Big Moose?"

"I did. My brother was very impressed with the service. He told me about the Irish family saved by your husband's people. Very brave."

"It all started at Big Moose, right?" I ask.

"Well, the strange thing was that he started saying it differently. Let me think. It was something like 'it all ends at Big Moose', or, wait, here it is, 'It's all in the end Big Moose." Quiet descends, we all look at each other, trying to figure it out.

"Do you still have contact with Big Moose?" I ask.

"Oh, yes. We have a camp up there, we spent all our summers there when the boys were young."

"How about recently?"

"We'd go up for the odd weekend. Ken went up on his own one time to meet a logger. There were some trees we were afraid would come down on the cabin. We had them removed."

Yvette looks at me and I know we're both thinking the same thing.

58

Warehouse Row, New York

The air is chilly. The sun is just starting to peak over the roofs of the easternmost row of warehouses. Max and Jonny are sitting with their backs to one of the walls, paper bags with bottle in hand.

They're around the corner from Boris's place, out of sight from windows and cameras. This street is one that his vehicles must use to get in and out. Jonny stumbles out into the street as if looking to pick something up. Instead he puts something down. From where Max is it looks like a small pile of junk, the same as the hundreds of others that litter the area. Jonny stumbles back.

"Think it'll work?"

"Should. The launcher looks like all this other crap. Nobody's gonna think it's odd. I hit the trigger at the right time it'll shoot up and stick to the undercarriage. After that it tracks. We can look at it on the laptop later."

"Not bad. Not bad at all."

Jonny beams.

They settle in. Forty minutes later they hear them. Two blacked out SUVs exit the compound and turn the corner. Max and Jonny are out of sight, slumped along a sidewall. As the first vehicle passes over Jonny's tracker he hits the remote. Max can barely make it out as it goes airborne. It stays up. Seems they're in business. Hopefully later on they'll be able to learn a little more about Boris and his crew, where they go, what they do.

With that job done Jonny leads Max between a few of the metal sheds to a point where they can see the compound. A ten foot high chain link fence surrounds the building. Its only about twenty feet from the fence to the building. The sun glints on the razor sharp barbs of the concertina wire that tops the fence. On the roof are some communications units. The corners of the building have high def cameras.

"This is a serious operation, Jonny."

"I don't see anybody," Jonny says. "Think they all left in the SUVs?"

"If there's nobody home there will be electronic security," Max answers. "But nothing we can't handle."

"Don't see any dogs," Jonny murmurs.

"Good if there aren't. May be inside, though."

They move behind the buildings as quickly as they can until they're out of visual, then cross the street and work they're way back up to the rear of the warehouse. Standing with their backs flat against the wall Max steals a look.

"I don't see any movement behind the windows, but the camera's worry me a bit." He crouches and inches his head forward again, taking it all in.

"We can get through the fence, even if its hot. We get close to the building we can be out of camera view. Then we figure a way in."

That's when he hears the dogs, and they're on his side of the fence.

"Shit," says Jonny.

"Take it easy," Max says. "Looks like we're getting in."

They stand with their backs to the fence. They stay still as the two Dobermans take up holding positions on either side of them. Two military types with AK-47's join the party.

"Hands on head. Face down." Their accents are thick but the intention is clear. Max and Jonny, with hands on top of their heads, sink to their knees, then face down. One of the men thoroughly frisks each of them while the other guard and the two dogs look on.

"Leave us alone, can't you. We don't hurt anyone, just take their bottles and cans," Max gives it a try. The quick kick in the ribs is the only answer he gets.

Plastic ties are used to bind their hands behind them, then they're pulled roughly to their feet. A shove with a rifle barrel and the group marches to the front of the building. One of the patrol enters a code, his body shielding the view from Max and Jonny. As the gate slides open Max whispers to Jonny, "We're in. That wasn't hard."

The warehouse door opens the same way.

No blindfolds. Getting out might not be on offer from the two captors.

Clean, neat and well lit, they are standing in a large steel structure, the cement floors gleaming. The farthest bay contains a large trash hauler. In the next bay sits a powerful looking Harley. The other two bays are empty. The side where Max and Jonny stand looks like two stories of rooms accessed by metal stairs. There's a smell of gasoline and disinfectant. And garbage. They're taken into a small room on the first floor.

"Sit. No talk."

A cell phone comes out and the man punches in a number. He speaks Russian and makes his report, listens, then barks his agreement to whatever order has been given. Max steals a look at Jonny and sees that his eyes are wide and his breathing fast. Jonny's scared shitless. Max looks at their captors. Black military type utilities, jungle boots, automatic weapons and side arms. They back out and lock the door. Max looks over at Jonny and smiles.

"Now we wait."

59

Road Trip to Big Moose

It's early morning when we get to Julia Dixon's house to pick her up. I put in a call to Greene. I want to know if I can get into my cabin, or if it's still a crime scene. There's some orienteering gear I want to pick up. He assures me it's OK and asks what's up. I explain that we're going to Big Moose looking for clues. He sounds a little concerned, but wishes us luck.

As we pull up to the trail to the cabin there's a familiar purple and gold state police cruiser parked there. A smiling trooper Murphy gets out and greets us.

"Greene called me," he explains. "Thought I might tag along, if that's OK?"

I introduce him to Yvette, Julia, and Reid. His gaze lingers on Yvette and Julia. Males can't help themselves, it seems. He gives Reid a questioning look.

"I work with Max," Reid explains. "He's mentioned you to me. Glad you're on board."

This is the most I've heard out of Reid. Murphy's smiling again. I leave them chatting and head up to the cabin and get my gear. By the time I get back its been decided that Murphy will leave his cruiser and travel with us in the SUV. I'm not sure, but I think his smile's gotten bigger. He takes a long satchel from his trunk and places it in the back alongside Reid's gear

Where we're headed isn't that far as the crow flies, but the mountains pretty much decide where the highways can go, and the circuitous route will take us about an hour. Luckily it's a beautiful day. Mid-seventies, the sun in a cloudless sky. Leaves can be seen turning to autumn colors in a few spots. I can't help but think it's a great day to be alive.

60

Warehouse Row, New York

Max hears a car door slam. The 'beep' from the keypad on the secure front door of the warehouse goes off. That door slams. Now there are footsteps on the metal stairs. Shoes, not heavy boots like the guards. The footsteps go past the room they're in, go to the second floor. A lock turns, a door opens and closes. Faint footsteps walking around up there. Next the command comes down. Russian again. They're to be brought up. Max is pretty sure it's just the new guy and the two guards here with him and Jonny.

"Up," growls the guard, roughly giving them some help.

Out the door and up the stairs, muzzles on them the whole way. The open door leads into a modern, well furnished, office. Heavy, dark wood desk with a laptop open on it. Matching credenza and file cabinets. A pile carpet covers the cement floor. It's the man that catches Max's interest. About five ten, swarthy, dark hair slicked back. Eyes a little too close together. The suit and shoes real expensive, Italian most likely. Starched white shirt, blue silk tie.

The man points to the two hard backed chairs arranged in the middle of the room. The guards push them down onto them, hands still cabled behind them. The man then goes to the front of his desk and leans back on it. He takes a gleaming stiletto from a drawer, passing it from one hand to the other. He looks at one of the guards and tells him in Russian to get back on watch.

"Drop any pretense you might be considering," English now. "I want names, what you are doing here, who you work for, what you think you know." He smiles. Jonny is hyperventilating.

Out of the corner of his eye Max sees the remaining guard has relaxed some since his boss has taken over. His rifle is slung around his

161

neck with both his hands in front of him, his wrists resting on stock and barrel.

"We don't know nothin'," Max states. "Just lookin' for cans."

Boris laughs as he walks around and half sits on the front of the desk.

"Oh, you know something, and you will tell me. Be sure of that." He walks back behind the desk. "Maybe I'll start with the little man."

A new odor joins the mix. Poor Jonny. Max decides its time to finish up. Each movement takes no more than a tenth of a second. He jumps off the chair, feet high, bringing his hands under and up in front of him. Before the guard can straighten Max has the barrel end of the AK-47 in his two bound hands. Two tenths gone. In a blur of motion, as if turning a large crank, Max rotates the rifle. Once. Twice. The sling around the guard's neck tightens quickly. Three times and the guard slumps as his neck snaps. As the para drops Max relieves him of his pistol. At the half second mark Max stops Boris progress with the knife by putting the pistol muzzle to his forehead.

"New plan," says Max. "Drop the knife. I've got some questions of my own." He looks to Jonny, whose sitting open mouthed. "Use the knife to cut the ties. Don't get between us."

Jonny disentangles the automatic rifle from around the dead commando's neck. Just then they hear the gates rolling open. Max peeks out. Their other captor is rolling back the entrance gate. A large Lincoln SUV has pulled up outside. Max watches as the SUV's back doors open. Two black clad paras exit each side of the vehicle and adopt a loose formation by the warehouse door. The front passenger door opens and another large man dressed in black gets out. He walks around to the driver's window. He leans in, appearing to have some discussion with the driver. When the soldier stands upright and steps back the SUV drives off. Max steps back from the window, letting the blind fall into place.

"What now, big man?" The suit smiles that smile, the one Max doesn't like.

Max whips him across the face with the pistol, breaking his nose and knocking out a couple of those perfect teeth. Probably weren't originals, Max tells himself. He can hear the troops in the ready room below. Someone is clumping up the stairs.

It's all broken English now. They must be told to practice. The para is outside the door. Two sharp raps. No response from inside the room. Max has Boris' arms locked behind him with one hand as the other shoves the gun barrel into his neck. Blood runs freely from the Boss's nose and mouth, covering the starched white shirt, creating interesting designs on the blue silk tie. Across from the dead para's body Jonny is doing something at the desk.

"Teams two and three are in motion, Boss." The para waits a beat for Boris to answer. "Have you instructions for Team one?" He waits. "Boss? Anatoly? You have prisoners?" The para is unsure and increasingly unhappy. "Boss, have you instructions for Team one?"

"I have instructions for you, asshole," Max responds, the command voice leaving no doubt whose in charge inside the room. "Anatoly is dead." He lets this sink in for a beat. "Your Boss is next." Another beat. "Unless you do as I say. Anybody feels like a hero, he dies. Stack your weapons and form up in the empty bay." Max looks back to Boris, whose face is inches away, and forces the gun further into his throat, his meaning clear.

"Do as he says," Boris instructs, his broken teeth affecting his voice, even more evidence that the balance of power inside the compound has changed. The para issues the necessary orders and they hear troops moving into place.

Max looks over at Jonny. "Can you drive that Harley?"

"Oh yeah," Jonny smiles.

"Let's get out of here," Max nods his head toward the door. Jonny steps over Anatoly and opens it. The para stands on the metal landing, takes in Max, the gun stuck in Boris' neck, the dead para on the floor. The rest appear to be in the truck bay as directed. Max indicates with his head and the para turns and starts down the metal stairs.

Max does a quick headcount. Comes out right. They hadn't expected trouble at home. Still he has Jonny go first, checking.

The six ex-soldiers stand in a rough formation in the spotless truck bay, the cement at their feet still gleaming. They watch Max carefully with sideways glances.

"EYES FRONT!" he commands. They obey instantly. To the para from upstairs, "Open the bay doors and the gate." The man moves to a panel next to the entrance and soon the rumble of chains and clank of wheels fills the dead silence. The roar of Jonny firing up the Harley takes over, the smell of exhaust filling the space.

Max walks Boris to the bike, throws his leg over behind Jonny, then pulls Boris sidesaddle in front of him. He whispers to Jonny, "Take it slow, Jonny. I fall off and we're through."

Jonny does. They rumble past the ex-soldiers and out of the bay, over the crushed stone of the drive and through the gate. Jonny swoops to the right and throttles up a bit, now clear of the compound and on the street.

Max looks back and sees the paras watching. They're unsure what to do. Suddenly his solar plexus explodes in pain and he has all he can do to hang on to Jonny. The elbow punch also projects Boris away, bouncing along the road next to them for a second, then rolling off to the side in a puff of dust. Gunfire from the warehouse starts slowly, picks up as the weapons are retrieved. Jonny guns it around a corner.

61

Adirondack Mountains Near Big Moose

I feel the bumps shoot right up my spine, even in the high riding Chevy. Murphy rides up front with Reid, our de facto protectors.

"How much further, Julia?" We've been off the main highway for about ten minutes, taking it slow, winding around the potholes where we can.

"See those two small hills up ahead? We go between them and then it levels out down to the camp. Maybe another ten minutes."

It's been a pleasant drive. The scenery is great, and Julia is an interesting and vivacious conversationalist. She and her husband had wide ranging interests, traveled a lot. Reid, always capable, doesn't say much. I ask him about Max, though, and he provides a surprising insight.

"Max isn't taking to 'retirement' too well. Your problems are just what he needs right now. I just worry that he might take too many risks."

"What's that mean?"

Reid looks at me, then back to the road. "Max never figured on dying in bed."

I get a chill at that. Reid isn't inclined to say any more, so I let it go.

All in all, I feel pretty good, and I'm hopeful that we find something to help us solve the mystery of Ken's death. We pass between the two hills and the view opens up. About a mile down I see a clearing with a small cabin. There're a few pine trees, and a dock that runs out into the bluest water I think I've ever seen. I can make out one or two small outbuildings. We're almost there.

62

Bronx, New York

Max and Jonny are back at his hidey-hole. Max is making a couple of sandwiches while Jonny showers and changes his clothes. Max tries Mann's cell phone but it goes right to voice mail. Out of range he figures, up where they are. Jonny comes in the room, grabs a beer and a sandwich and sits down by his computer.

"Gonna see where Boris's other playmates went off to?" Max asks.

"The maps are loading now. I'll have to zoom out, I don't see anything around here." Turns out Jonny has to zoom way out before he picks up the signal from his little toy. "Got 'em."

Max watches as Jonny hunkers over his computer screen. The map of New York State changes to focus on an area north of the Mohawk River. The screen becomes an area of green, dotted with blue 'map' lakes, and a single highway snaking through it. There's a blinking pixel on that highway. Jonny makes some adjustments using the onscreen navigation, and soon the map identifies the area as the Moose River Basin.

"Oh shit!" Max is barely audible, pointing at the screen. "That's where Mann and Yvette are headed. Julia Dixon's camp at Big Moose."

"Those guys must be right on top of them," Jonny says as he navigates closer, more detail on the monitor.

They can see that the SUV is a short distance away from the turnoff from 28N onto the only road that leads down to the plains.

"We've got to warn them," Max says. "They won't have a chance."

Jonny looks up at Max, says "Is there a land line? Cause there's no cell coverage up there."

Max shakes his head 'No', pulls out his cellphone and punches in a number.

"FBI, Albany. How can I direct your call?"
"Give me Greene, now!"

63

Albany County Jail

Jimmy Smith stands with his back to the wall by the entrance to the lunch hall. His hands hang off the duty belt as he slowly rocks back and forth on the balls of his feet. He still looks like the pretty good high school athlete he'd been two years earlier. Never had college potential. Just wasn't that smart. Wanted to be a cop, where his size and strength would give him an advantage. He also liked to push people around. He guessed he was what they called a bully and got all upset about. He didn't understand. Couldn't get on the force, though, even with his uncle a big shot detective. The tests were tough. His uncle got him a job at the jail, though, and it seemed to him that this was as good as it was going to get. He didn't mind it too much. He wore a uniform, and could pretty much do whatever he wanted to the scum that he dealt with every day. He even took a little bit of pride in that he thought he did a good job.

The sergeant strides by, tapping the face of the large metal watch he wore like a medal. "Smith, get 'em in to eat, and make sure there's no trouble."

"You bet Sarge, no problem."

Jimmy was pretty sure the sergeant didn't like him, gave him shit details, waiting for him to fuck up.

The sergeant stops and comes back to Jimmy Smith.

"That Russian that came in last night bothers me. Doesn't make sense, what he did. Keep an eye on him. Beat a guy up in front of the police station. No robbery, no provocation. Like he wanted to get arrested. Big fucker. Dead eyes, no emotion." The sergeant looks in Jimmy's face for some sign of cognition.

"Don't you worry, Sarge," Jimmy reassures.

The dining hall is just a large concrete room with a kitchen along one long wall and a serving line in front of it. The tables are bolted to the floor, stainless steel. The benches are the same. On one end of the serving line are stacks of plastic trays, paper plates, and some fucked up plastic thing that serves as a spoon and a fork. No knives of any sort.

Forty five men trudge through a door on the other side of the room from Jimmy. Two guards usher them in. There are ten guards in total, and they circle the prisoners like wolves, full of attitude and menace. As the prisoners collect their trays and move into the food line Jimmy moves to a position at the far end of the line, adjusting the truncheon and pepper spray on his belt. He checks his taser. Charged and ready.

Jimmy looks for the Russian the sergeant warned him about. Finds him standing with a tray in his hand, taking his time getting into line. Finally Jimmy sees him slide in behind that nervous shit, Broner. Jimmy has to smirk. There was a loser. Caught red-handed topping a state cop of some sort. FBI would be taking him off their hands. They might fry the fucker. Jimmy watches them work their way down the line. Potatoes. Peas. Something that passes for meat in this place. Gravy with a slick sheen on it. Broner and the Russian are almost through. Jimmy watches Broner reach out for some stale bread. Then he sees it. Somehow the Russian has a shiv in his hand. Jimmy lets out a roar and rushes him as he sees the shiv go in and out of Broner at least two times.

Broner screams and drops to the floor. He crabs away as Jimmy grabs the Russian. Now the shiv is going in and out of Jimmy as the big man holds him up with his free hand. Mayhem ensues. The other deputies panic and start pushing prisoners out of the way as they rush to where Jimmy now lies on the floor, hands trying to stop the flow of his own blood. The Russian stands next to him, head bowed, shiv on the floor in front of him.

The first deputy has his baton cocked as he runs up to the Russian. The first blows make flat squishy sounds.

Eventually they club the crazy bastard senseless.

Broner is declared critical, bundled up and rushed to the hospital under heavy security.

Jimmy is declared dead.

64

Big Moose

We decided to search for an hour or so before digging into the lunch basket Julia and Yvette had put together. The two women were going through the cabin, taking out drawers, emptying closets, looking over and under anything that caught their eye. I was outside with Murphy turning the shed upside down while Reid prowled around the kayaks, tree stumps, rocks, and dock.

Murphy had brought his satnav phone into the cabin and left it on the table. I was beginning to feel the heat of the sun, starting to break a sweat, when Yvette leaned out the cabin door and called to Murphy.

"Sergeant, your phone's making a funny noise."

Murphy looked up, smiled and headed for the cabin. He came out a second later holding the device, looking for the best signal he could get. Going back to my shed clearing I couldn't help but think of all the happy times the Dixon's had probably shared in this idyllic spot.

A movement caught my attention and I looked back towards Sergeant Murphy. The Trooper was outside the cabin door, still on the wooden deck, waving his arm at me, indicating to go inside. Then he ran off to get Reid's attention.

When I entered the cabin I saw that Yvette and Julia were still working their way around the various potential hiding places, apparently unaware of whatever was bothering Murphy.

"Something's up," I told them. "Murphy's on the phone. He had me come in."

Both women stopped their labor, Yvette stepping down off a chair she was using to check the top of a bookcase, Julia getting off her knees from inspecting a cabinet. They came to where I was standing, and we all turned to the door, waiting for Murphy.

Out the back window I could see Murphy and Reid. Murphy finished with the phone and put it back in its case. He and Reid had a short conversation and jogged back to the cabin. I had a bad feeling in the pit of my stomach, which only got worse when I saw the grim look on the faces of the two men as they entered the cabin. Murphy looked at Reid, who nodded, telling him to go ahead. He looked at each of us before he spoke.

"Long story," he started. "No time for details. There's two SUV's like the ones that visited you at your cabin coming down the road towards us. We need to get out of here." I stood there with Yvette and Julia, unable to comprehend that this beautiful setting, the pines and blue water and hundred year old cabin were under threat from the people that killed Julia's husband.

The sun poured in through the windows at the front of the cabin, warm on our flesh, a cool breeze through the open door. Birds were still calling outside, and the water lapped against the dock. What Murphy had just said seemed so bazaar, so unreal.

We watched as the two duffel bags, one Reid's, one Murphy's, were opened on the table. Kevlar vests were handed out. Murphy and Reid each extracted rifles, shouldered the duffels and waved us outside. Murphy and Reid had apparently arrived at a basic plan between the dock and the cabin.

Murphy led us down to the plank dock while Reid followed us. He got into the water where it was about knee deep, motioned us to do the same and started off inside the water's edge. The water was cool on my legs, and even at knee depth was a struggle to move through. Even so, we went fairly fast, and more quietly that I would've thought. We made it around a small headland and Murphy seemed to relax a little. Apparently being caught at the cabin would have been a disaster for us. I didn't feel that we were much better off, but was also happy to let Murphy and Reid figure it out.

After about ten minutes we came to a rock strewn area where a small streambed, now mostly dry, came in.

"We'll follow this," Murphy announced. "Stay on the rocks and try not to disturb them. Don't worry about wet footprints, the sun will dry them in minutes."

He started up the mild incline made by the streambed, with Julia, Yvette and me following. Reid was a ways back, checking for pursuers I assumed. We were able to follow this for about a quarter mile, if my experience judging distances from jogging was close. Apparently the direction was satisfactory to Murphy – away from the camp and the road in. I was starting to sweat now, even though we were under the cool canopy of the trees. We came to an area that flattened out and opened up. Murphy called a halt and I gratefully sat on a rock and caught my breath, watching Yvette and Julia do the same. Reid caught up and he and Murphy had a quick consult.

"Who knew that you were planning to go to the cabin?" Murphy asked.

We looked at each other for a moment. "Max and Greene," I said.

"Who talked to them? And from where?"

"I did," I said. "I called Max from Julia's house yesterday, and Greene from there this morning."

"Was Max on his cell?"

"No, I caught him at the house, I used the landline." Murphy and Reid exchanged knowing glances.

"I'll scout a spot," Reid said and took off up the trail.

"What's going on," Yvette demanded of Murphy.

"We figure that they somehow managed to put a trace on your home phone."

"That's how they know that we're here," Julia said in a whisper.

Murphy nodded. "They wouldn't know about me, though, and probably not about Reid. That's an advantage."

"An advantage for what?" I ask.

Murphy took a second to look each of us in the eye.

"The ambush."

65

Bronx, New York

Max Bobo was fit to be tied. Jonny watched him pace like a cornered lion. Shit was going down on people he swore he'd protect, and he was nowhere near the action. He couldn't fuckin' believe it. The cell didn't finish the first ring by the time Max had it to his ear.

"Well?" he demanded.

"I got a hold of Murphy on his sat-phone. No contact yet. He and Reid are going to take evasive action, try to get clear ASAP."

"Weapons?"

"Murphy has a pump action and an AR. Reid says he has the usual. Handguns, of course." Max smiled in spite of the serious situation. Reid's 'usual' could take out an infantry platoon. Has.

"Back-up?"

"State Police have a chopper in the air. The 10th Mountain Division has two Black hawks fired up. At best, thirty minutes out." Too long, Max thought, too long.

"Thanks Greene. Keep me posted." He clicked the cell off and looked helplessly at Jonny. "We wait."

66

Ambush Site, Adirondack Mountains

I can feel the damp earth on my stomach as I lay in the flat space under the hanging roots. Reid found the spot he liked. Murphy liked it too. I'm terrified. My heart is racing and I have to really concentrate on my breathing. I keep monitoring and telling myself that I'm in no danger, not right now. When the action starts I'll be all right. Please God!

The belief is that they'll be coming uphill towards our position. Reid is pretty sure they'll employ what he called 'flank security', that they'll be a little worried about our escape route.

"How will they find us?" Yvette had asked. "Between the water and the rocks and hard packed soil we've left no tracks."

"That's exactly it, and why they'll be worried. When they realize there are no tracks, they'll do what we did, what they'd do in our spot. That will bring them here."

The blowdown that tightened the trail had also uprooted a stand of white birch near the top of the hill. We were lying in the cave-like depression made when the trees went over, the birch lying in a tangle over the crest of the small hill. On our side an opening was created where we could lay flat under the dirt and root system, with small bushes taking root along the rim in front of us helping hide our presence. Reid said the rock and dirt would protect us from their fire, and to keep down when not shooting. Each of us had a 'vector'. Reid was going to take the front. He had some major guns and grenades. Yvette and I had our left, Murphy and Julia our right. I had a 12-gauge auto reload shotgun. Reid loaded it with slugs, showed me how to point and shoot, told me anything I hit would go down, no worries.

"You ever shot before?"

"Not since I was a kid, and not well then."

"You'll be fine, Mann." He turned his attention to Yvette, who was sighting along a 30.06 rifle. "How about you?"

"Used to have a boyfriend who took me shooting. He stopped when it became obvious I was much better at it."

"OK. Julia?"

"Military Police during Gulf 1. Met Ken there."

Reid and Murphy grinned at each other. "Get comfy. We'll know when they come."

The plan was for each of us to pick up our target as soon as they appeared. Mine would be their man on my flank. Yvette would take the man inside him. Julia and Murphy would do the same on the other side. Reid would work on the rest. They'd given us language to use to update status, 'got mine', 'missed', 'incoming'. I've already forgotten the rest.

As I sighted along the barrel I noticed smoke curling into the air from back where we'd come from. Julia saw it too.

"Bastards, they're burning the camp." Her jaw was set, but I could see her eyes glisten.

We heard the plonk of a displaced rock somewhere below us, in the streambed.

"Here they come."

67

Bronx, New York

Max hears Boris' voice boom through the crowded space. He crouches and wheels around, empty pizza boxes flying, his glock pointed at Jonny's laptop. Jonny's office chair backpedals against the wall as Jonny holds his hands up in front of him. Eyes wide he points at his laptop.

"I left a bug in his office," he gasps. "Just getting to the recording."

Max takes a breath, a half smile forms as he shakes his head and slips the weapon into its holster. He sits down in the side chair and stares at Jonny. Jonny stares back, seems unsure what to do. Max breaks the silence.

"Lets see what we've got."

"OK," relieved, Jonny wheels his way back to the desk and hits the audio, makes some adjustments and Boris' voice comes back, clearly pissed off. The voice is loud and clear, but hard to understand.

"He's coming through a little rocky," Max says.

"Probably has something to do with his broken teeth."

Max tilts his head, dog like, close listening.

"Sounds like they're clearing out," Jonny says, looks at Max. "He's talking about two days from now picking up something. Or is he pushing something? Or is it Putin? Now he's talking about docks and a hotel."

Max just shakes his head, more important things on his mind.

"Keep trying to figure it out. I'm going to call Greene again, see what's happening."

68

Ambush Site, Adirondack Mountains

They came just as Reid said they would. Two on each side providing flank security, the other four hugging the sides of the trail, about a meter apart. I picked up my target and in my mind heard Reid's words, "Breath in, hold, and squeeze. Don't jerk or pull."

They were to get a lot closer. I kept my sight on my man and waited for Reid's command. Not a shout or a whisper. An even voiced command.

"Now!"

The world exploded. I pulled, rather than squeezed, the trigger. I saw a sapling snap in half behind my target, who quickly dropped to the ground out of sight. Shots started to ring out in front of us. I heard Yvette's voice next to me, "Got mine." Rounds were hitting the dirt and roots over my head, kicking up dirt around the rim in front of us. "Mine down," reported Julia and Murphy in one voice.

The return fire was growing in intensity. Reid raised up, one knee on the ground. I saw the grenade in his hand. He pulled the pin and lobbed it down the hill, an explosion, a scream. He was already grabbing another one from his belt. This time as he rose up and pulled the pin he was knocked back, a red stain spreading on his arm. He still had the grenade in his hand, which he threw overhand. It cleared the rim and rolled down the hill, exploding a second later. There was silence from below now. Murphy and I crawled to the forward rim, pointing our guns down the hill. Nobody was moving. I saw a lot of blood. An arm off to the side all by itself. A man groaning, or was he crying.

Julia and Yvette were on either side of Reid. They dragged him to the rear of our little space and opened his shirt. At the same time I saw

Murphy gesturing to me. "Cover me," he mouthed, and disappeared from the shelter, headed up the hill. Looking for the guy I missed. I wasn't sure how to cover him from where I was, under the earth while he was circling around it. Then a bit of dirt fell in front of me. I checked my shotgun. Good to go. Slowly I stepped out from the shelter, looking up.

There he was, working his way along the upper rim of the blowdown. He had his rifle in hand, grenade with pin in clenched in his teeth, the other hand holding on to the tangle of trees as he worked his way over our dugout.

As I stepped out he spotted me. He contorted his body to fire a shot that went wild. Slowly I raised my gun, pointed it up his ass, took a breath, held it, and squeezed the trigger.

He lifted off the dirt face he was scrambling across and stayed motionless in midair for a full second. Then he fell at my feet, the top of his head gone. The grenade rolled harmlessly down the hill, the pin still in.

"GOT MINE!"

* * *

Murphy and I were checking the casualties. I did what Murphy instructed, approached cautiously, weapon at the ready. Look for signs of life and location of weapons. Feel the carotid artery, at the throat, at the side of the Adam's apple, for any sign of a pulse. Hold the back of the hand over the mouth, see if you feel any breath. If they're still alive call him, if not, collect their guns and move on. The only other dead man I'd been this close to was Ken Dixon, but I hadn't touched him.

The man Yvette shot was in the heavy brush and uprooted trees on the same hill as our ambush, a little lower down. He was draped over some storm ravaged saplings. Not moving. I felt a little breeze on my face as I moved closer to him. An automatic rifle lay in the brush under him, his body supported by the saplings. I was aware that my vision had tunneled as I got closer to him. The terrain was difficult to maneuver in, so I had to take my time. Finally I could reach out and touch him. Whereas a second before my breathing was rapid, now I couldn't breathe at all.

I grabbed his shoulder, some kind of strap or harness, and rolled him away from me. Even though I'd caused his movement, I was still startled when it happened. He turned onto his back, legs tangled in the brush, more like a rag doll than the fearsome commando of five minutes before. I had a quick jolt when I saw that his eyes were open. I reached out with two shaking fingers and closed them. Why? Too many movies, I thought. Then I put my fingers at his throat, because Murphy said to. Then the back of my hand over his mouth, cause Murphy said to. Nothing. I gathered his weapons and moved on.

Murphy had a live one, the man Julia shot. He hogtied him and moved on. I got to the grenade victims just as one of them died. His body looked cut in half. When I bent over him his eyes focused on me briefly, then the light faded until just a dull fog remained. As I stared at the man I became conscious of a dull 'wump, wump'.

Choppers were coming. We gathered and stared up as the noise grew. Two Blackhawks entered our vision, hovering overhead. Murphy stepped into an opening in the trees and began signaling them in. The sky seemed to fill with snakes as eight ropes exploded into the blue sky from the sides of the copters, immediately followed by battle ready soldiers fast roping from each chopper. They were among us in battle formation in seconds.

The 10th Mountain team checked all the casualties again, just to be sure, while their medic took a look at Reid. Yvette and Julia had been trying to staunch the bleeding at Reid's left arm with cloth ripped from their shirttails. The medic pulled the makeshift bandages away and cut off Reid's shirt.

"Wow." He whistled softly. "This wasn't your first bullet, was it buddy?"

Reid had a variety of scars all over his torso. A couple could be identified as bullets, others looked like they might have come from a knife. The rest? Shrapnel? Reid didn't even know.

"You're lucky, clean through. I can stop the bleeding, treat the wound with antibiotic, and put your arm in a sling. I recommend medevac to an ER, and a night of monitoring. What do you say?"

Reid just smiled.

The combat medic laughed and shook his head.

"What I thought. Humor me and keep the sling on until I'm gone, will ya?"

"He'll keep the sling on," Julia and Yvette said in one voice, as Reid looked at them, mildly amused.

The medic repacked his bag and stuck his hand out. Reid took it in a firm handshake.

"It's an honor to meet you, Colonel." He was gone.

"Colonel?" the two women said in unison.

"What is it with you two? Borg?" Just then Murphy walked up. He'd been talking with the soldiers, using their com unit.

"What now?" Reid asked, back to business.

"The sergeant is arranging transport for us. We'll walk to the LZ, back by the cabin. A State Police chopper will get us and we'll be back in Albany in no time." He stretched. "Best thing we can do right now is relax, deal with what we just went through. I need to get a heads up from Greene. Then we'll move out."

We sat in our makeshift ambush site, now a place sanctified by the firefight and the lives lost, and tried to collect ourselves as the enormity of what we had just been through hit us. I smelled the fresh dirt, saw the roots of the fallen birch hang down from above, and actually felt secure in this little haven. Julia came up and settled down next to me. Yvette was with her.

"I've never been so scared in my life," Julia said. Yvette nodded her head in agreement, looking at me, gauging my mental state after killing a man. I felt fine, even a little elated at having survived. I winked at her, she made a face and turned to hear what Julia was saying.

"This has always been such a peaceful getaway. All this violence, hard to get my head around it. I can't believe they burned the camp," she sighed, as the words tumbled out. "It really is the 'end of the moose' like Ken was saying."

We all sat silent and contemplated the sad words, the losses that kept mounting for this poor woman, the bravery she'd just shown. Men from the 10th Mountain worked their way around us, the occasional shouted order breaking the stillness.

"I want to visit the museum soon," Yvette broke the silence, tried to change the mood. "I want to sit in that glade, listen to the bird sounds, and feel the peace," she shuddered slightly as she spoke.

"The place where the moose is?" Julia looked up. I remembered Yvette telling me about it when we were in Ireland.

"Ken loved that place. He'd sit there waiting for the exhibit to empty, to be alone. He loved that moose," she laughed. "He'd walk right up and pat it on its flank."

Yvette gave me a questioning look, her head tilted to one side. No way. Murphy joined us then.

"OK, here's the deal. Just conferenced with Max and Greene. They want to keep this quiet until the police have processed the scene and the bodies. And questioned the survivor. They want us all to meet up back at the FBI office in Albany as soon as we can get there. Eli Massry, Broner's lawyer, is in town and Max wants him to join us." He looked at Julia. "It seems Broner got attacked in the prison, stabbed a couple of times but expected to recover. A deputy sheriff was killed in the attack." Murphy looked at me, "You're friend Detective Fendrick's nephew."

"So, looks like Boris was trying to clear the slate," I said. "These goons were going to take us out, while another one went after Broner."

"He's also missed on all counts," Reid pointed out.

I stood up, brushing the leaves and dirt off my jeans. We gathered what little we had and followed Murphy single file back towards the burned out cabin where the helicopter was waiting to take us back to the city.

69

New York State Thruway, Northbound

Max drove the red mustang north while Jonny worked his laptop.

"It's hard to hear, Jonny. Were those the cheapest bugs you could get?"

"Next to, but they'd still be OK if the fucker had all his teeth."

"You didn't complain when he lost them."

"No, that was one of the sweetest things I've ever seen," Jonny smiled and settled back, working the laptop. He frowned. "You won't tell anybody what happened, will you?"

"What, that we got jumped and fought our way out?"

"No," Jonny paused, embarrassed. "That I shit my pants."

Max laughed hard enough that Jonny was worried he might lose control of the car.

"Jonny, I've been in this line of work for well over forty years. We've all shit our pants. Those are the good times."

Jonny smiled. They rode in silence for a while.

"What now, Max?"

"I've got to meet up with the team, figure out where we are."

"I'm not on the team, am I Max?"

"It's a little delicate, Jonny. Besides the FBI and State Police, there's the widow of the man you helped kill. Now might not be the best time to bring you in." Max gave Jonny a sideways glance. "Right now I need you to do research on that tape. I might need you to send a copy to the FBI, if they'll touch it, considering it can't be used as evidence. You're my back room, Jonny. That's where I need you now."

Jonny settled back, the concern gone from his face. The laptop open on his lap, he copied the file for the FBI in case they wanted it, and went back to work cleaning up the audio. He started to try various permutations of the words he thought he heard, using Google to see if any made sense.

"Puccinia mean anything to you?" Jonny asked over the roar of the engine.

"No, why? Is it important?"

Jonny shrugged.

70

FBI, Albany, New York

Whatever the mysteries of time and travel, we all seemed to arrive at the Albany FBI headquarters at about the same time. Five of us were travelling together of course. Greene was already there. Max had just driven up from New York and stashed Jonny in a motel nearby. Eli Massry, who Max had met, but the rest of us didn't know, had just come from visiting his client at the hospital.

Greene ushered us into a large conference room with a round table in the center. Along the sidewall were comfortable looking chairs, a set up for coffee, tea, and soft drinks, and various bits and pieces of computer gear. He made the introductions.

"This is Eli Massry, he's Jason Broner's attorney. Lest you think differently, he has very little interest in Jason Broner other than as a conduit to bringing major pain to the people who hired him." Greene went on to introduce the others to Massry, who shook hands with Max Bobo and said, "You've developed quite an army, Mr. Bobo."

"You've no idea, Mr. Massry."

"Eli."

"Max."

And so it went. Each of us got our beverage of choice, if it was available, and took a seat at the table.

Greene got started. "Max was with Jonny, the guy Broner used as a tail, when they got picked up by men outside of Boris Sarnow's warehouse. I'll keep this short. They managed to escape. In the process Mr. Sarnow suffered several serious injuries. One of his men was killed."

Max ignored the looks he was getting, staying focused on Greene's recital.

"The purpose of their visit was for Jonny to plant a GPS device on Boris' fleet. They accomplished this, and when they got back to Jonny's living quarters found out that the SUV they'd tagged was en route to the cabin at Moose River."

A murmur went around the room. I'm sure everyone had been wondering, as I was, how they'd found out about Boris's troops trailing us to the woods. Also, we now knew without doubt that these were Boris's, that he was behind the attempt on our lives. Reid spoke up.

"We figure he somehow had an external tap on the phone at the house. When Mann called Max for an OK they would have heard about him, Yvette and Julia. They didn't know about me and Murphy. That gave us a significant advantage, cause they wouldn't know about our weapons either. Of course, that heads up gave us the chance to prepare. Those goons were expecting fish in a barrel."

I couldn't help it, sitting there, hearing those words, a shudder went through me. It scared me more than sitting on that hill, waiting for a target.

"Thanks for sending the cavalry, Agent Greene," Yvette said. Greene smiled.

"The cavalry didn't come from my guys, I'm sorry to say. They don't see a case here. Blinders still on. The State Police scrambled because of Sergeant Murphy. The 10th Mountain lads came along because of Colonel Reid. Seems they worked some of the same neighborhoods over in Afghanistan. They think a lot of him."

"This Jonny has been a big help, how'd he wind up working with Broner?" asked Murphy.

"I can answer that," Ely Massry joined in. "Broner used him for tailing his victims." He looked at Julia. "Sorry, Mrs. Dixon. Broner wanted to know the habits of his victims. He hired Jonny to sort them out. He also used him to find out whom he was working for. Said that was a type of insurance. Probably why they want him dead."

"What else can you tell us about him, Eli?"

"Max, I don't want to be insensitive with Mrs. Dixon in the room."

"It's all right, Mr. Massry. My husband's been murdered and I shot a man today. I think I can take it. But thanks." Eli nodded.

"Well, where your husband was concerned, Carson…"

"What?" said Reid.

"That's right. Jonny Carson, no 'H'. Hard to believe." Massry sighed and looked at Julia again. "I suppose there wasn't really that much. Broner knew that Mr. Dixon parked in the lot behind the museum, and that he went through the museum to get to it. There were a number of days when he would linger in the museum. Broner wanted one of those days so that there would be fewer people around."

I found Yvette looking at me again, her head at that same angle. I had stopped listening to Massry, was trying to look into her mind, when Greene's voice got sharp. "What day did he track them to Alex Bay?" Massry answered as best he could and Greene rushed out of the room. "Be right back."

I looked at Yvette, my brow furrowed. She looked at me, wide eyes saying, "Why are you so stupid?" I had no answer. Eli Massry reached out and put his hand over Julia's, his look saying he was in this because they take everything that's good from us. She nodded back, no need for words. Max, Reid and Murphy had just started talking about the firefight when Greene came back with some papers in his hand. He sat down and looked through them, glasses on the end of his nose. He looked up.

"Houston, we've got a problem," he was shaking his head. "Its all pretty clear now, but you needed Jonny to put all the little bits together."

"What's that, Greene?" Max was impatient. Greene took a deep breath.

"We got a report from the Canadian Mounties. They were investigating an explosion on the St. Lawrence, a houseboat, six young men died. They found a similar one had been in the area. Talked to the couple, émigré's from the Ukraine. Had been threatened into delivering an aluminum suitcase to an island. Saw the other boat burning the next day, figured it was supposed to be them. The day they delivered the suitcase, Boris was up there."

Stunned, we sat there. All I could think was, "Can this get any worse?" International terrorism. A bomb in a suitcase. In New York? It was Max who spoke first.

"What do they think was in the case?" Greene looked at him, his head moving up and down.

"Not a suitcase nuke. Too light."

Max nodded. "I think I know what it is." Greene's mouth fell open. The rest of us just stared at him.

"Chalk up another one for Jonny. That office bug, it was hard to make out, mostly cause I'd knocked out a few of Mr. Sarnow's teeth by that time, but Jonny went to work on it. I can have him send a copy of the file to you, Greene. Boris was talking about *puccinia*. It's deadly rusk, kills cereals and grains."

Greene was shaking his head, disbelieving. "So what?"

"I'm waiting for a friend to call back from CDC. Back in the '70s they were trying to weaponize it. Took an international treaty to make everybody stop. Some folks figure the Russians never did."

Greene sat back. He looked troubled. "Have Jonny send me the files, OK?" he asked Max, then settled back, his eyes staring out the windows, unseeing. He sat like this for a while, like the rest of us letting this new development sink in. What other twists and turns were ahead.

Greene's attention was drawn to Yvette and I saw her giving him the head to the side, 'don't you see it?' treatment. He stood and stretched and walked to the coffee stand in the corner of the room. I watched my sister follow him. Their heads were together for a while, his bobbing up to take a good look at her. Was that disbelief? They conferred for a while longer, Yvette seemed to be laying out some argument that he was beginning to accept, judging by the new direction his head was moving.

Greene looked over at Max, seemed to make a decision. He glanced briefly at Julia. He and Yvette returned to the table, cups in hand. When they sat down Greene cleared his throat to get everyone's attention.

"Well, we could have a real break here, a surprising development. I think Yvette should tell you."

I turned along with everyone else to stare at my sister. Her eyes were wide and her lips were pursed. This was going to be important.

"Yvette, have you got something?" Max asked.

She took a deep breath.

"I'm pretty sure I know where Kenneth Dixon hid the files."

71

New York State Museum, Albany, New York

We were at the museum in minutes, driving to the back towards a series of loading docks. We were all there. At first there had been incredulity at Yvette's conclusion. The more we thought about it, the more it made sense. Max called Jonny and grilled him about the times Ken Dixon had lingered at the museum, heard that he'd stay until he could have some time alone there, even the curators gave him space, made it hard for Jonny to keep an eye on him, from being too obvious. Julia sealed the deal when she said, "That would be Ken."

We pulled into a large utility area and got out. I saw two men standing by an elevator, one about fifty, wearing a sport coat and tie, the other probably in his twenties. The younger man had dark, curly hair and thick glasses. He was wearing a white smock.

"There's our welcoming committee," Greene said as he spotted them.

Greene showed his credentials. The older of the two introduced himself as the Head Curator and identified the man with him as the Senior Exhibit Technician. Greene didn't bother to introduce anyone other than himself.

The Curator was gruff as he greeted us. "I hope this isn't some kind of joke, Agent," he looked down at the card in his hand. "Greene."

Greene handed the Head Curator the Search Warrant he'd obtained. The man seemed to study it for longer than necessary, showing once again that the museum wasn't too pleased with this request. The Head Curator finished his review of the document and waved us to follow him into the elevator, which took us all to the exhibit space on the ground floor of the building. As we entered the Museum I noticed that the changing exhibit space in the front currently featured the Hudson River School of artists. The Curator guided us past the 9/11 exhibit, which brought a lump to my throat.

"Never forget," I said to myself.

We passed through an open area with glass enclosed presentations of the various birds found in the mountains, from bald eagles to hummingbirds, most featured in their native environs. As we entered the area constructed to replicate a mountain meadow, complete with pond, I could hear the familiar sounds of loons and coyotes mixed in with a myriad of other woodland creatures. Deer fed on tree bark, bobcats hovered on branches, prepared to lunge. There in the center of the room stood the moose. I couldn't help but wonder again at the size of the animal.

The Head Curator glowered as the exhibit technician put on a pair of blue latex gloves. They both looked around, apparently not wanting other museum visitors to witness what they were about to do. It was a quiet day.

The technician approached the back of the moose with such a serious expression that I almost started to laugh. I covered my mouth with my hand and refused to look at Yvette. The small man reached up and lifted the stuffed animal's tail, which was above his eye level. Moving as if he were defusing a bomb, the tech slowly inserted his thumb and two fingers into the rectal cavity. A confused look came over his face as he pulled his hand back out. He turned to Greene with a surprised look. His arm was extended, palm up, clearly displaying the jewel case containing what looked like a computer disc. I looked over at Yvette now, and saw a satisfied expression on my sister's pretty face.

Greene had the tech carefully place the case in an evidence bag he produced, gave the curator a receipt, and waved us all back toward the elevator. Neither the Head Curator nor the Senior Exhibit Technician moved from where they'd been standing. My last view of them, they were next to the big moose, looking very confused.

Back in the suburban the mood was positive.

"I'll bring this to our techs right away," Greene announced. "It won't take them long to find out what's on this disc."

72

FBI, Albany, New York

Max's cellphone went off. The Marine Corps Hymn. We were sitting around Greene's conference table. The techs were somewhere working on Ken Dixon's disk and on the file Jonny had sent over. We were at that exhausting stage where the body and mind recover from extreme activity, the numbness of inactivity. Max pulled his phone off his belt and looked at the screen. I saw his eyebrows go up. He saw us watching him, held up a finger and crossed the room to sit in one of the corner chairs.

"Jonathan, thanks for getting back to me."

"Good to hear your voice, Max. Social call?" said the genial voice in Atlanta. Jonathan Brennan was one of the top scientists at CDC. He'd worked with Max before on projects neither could talk about.

"You know better, Jon."

"Give me the facts."

"Aluminum suitcase smuggled across the Canadian border last week. 'Feels light' they said."

"Size of suitcase, country of origin?"

"Mid-size is the best we can get. Here's the problem. Probably Russia. Mafiya involvement likely. Some evidence of Spetsnaz and Chechen on this side."

Silence. Some pencil scratching.

"Weight and volume don't speak to a serious threat. Too light for nuke, not enough volume for anthrax. Any thoughts as to what it might be?"

"Some intel indicates something called puccinia."

"Oh my," exhaled Brennan.

Max's heart sank. He looked out at the six pairs of eyes fixed on his. "No science, Jon. Just tell me."

"A little history first. In 1972 the governments of the world were privately as worried about bioterrorist threats as nuclear. One hundred and forty countries signed the Biological and Toxins Weapons Convention."

"Job done, right?"

Brennan chuckled. "Many figured the Soviets, and after them the Russians, weren't constrained in their efforts as a result of having signed the convention."

"So what if they did continue the program? What can a suitcase do? You said a suitcase of anthrax would have tolerable limits."

"Doesn't attack humans, Max. Attacks plants, cereals. Wheat mainly. It's a rusk. Normal plant epidemics have caused yield loses over the last decade of about 250 million bushels despite millions of dollars spent on fungicides."

Max stared across the room. All eyes on him.

"So, assume this stuff has been built up as much as you might surmise, on average, what would be the reach and the time frame of the crop destruction? And what percentage? No science, real English, OK?"

Brennan took a shuddered breath.

"From sea to shining sea, Max."

"The whole country?"

"In months, Max. Effectively one hundred percent."

The six sets of eyes now saw an emotion they never thought they'd see.

Max Bobo swallowed. Hard.

"We have to move on this, Max. No lone wolf stuff here. Too big."

"I'd love some help, Jon, but the government won't listen. All our clues come from a convicted felon, and they implicate a Wall Street name that Justice won't even talk to."

"Max, I trust you. You have to understand, though, that CDC has to get their hands on this stuff before there's any chance of its dispersal. Our world, the one we know, hangs in the balance. That stuff could turn the USA into a third world country – almost overnight. We go from the third largest producer and the largest exporter of wheat to zero."

A long pause.

"I promise to update you as soon as we know more. We think there's a transfer of the suitcase the day after tomorrow. We're trying to figure out where. We think that's the best chance we have to get the case. I want your people there when we do."

"I'll put a team together, ready to move. I'll need as much advance notice as you can give me to get us to where we have to be."

"Under the radar, Jon. I don't need some government official trying to call us off this search, or take it over. They've been on the sidelines for so long they'll want to justify it, there isn't time."

"Under the radar, Max. Like always."

Max slowly put down the now silent cell phone, and looked around the room.

"We've got to find this thing."

* * *

"I have this cleaned up as much as possible. Max really fucked up this guys speech." Greene realizes he'd just sworn in front of the women, blushes. "Here we go. The best my folks can come up with is that the 'docs' are going to be 'traded' at eleven. Somebody named Peabody is involved. In two days. Day after tomorrow."

Julia sits half way down the shiny table across from me. I see her head tilt to the side, her eyes narrow and her lips purse. A small smile starts to flit across her lips. She coughs. Greene looks at her as if unhappy with the interruption. "Go ahead, I'm OK," she says.

Greene hits a key and the room fills with Boris' obviously altered voice, which is also obviously really, really angry. We listen. It means nothing to me. I look around. Yvette, who I'm betting on, seems perplexed. Murphy and Massry wear frowns, their brows furrowed. Julia looks nonplussed, patiently waiting for a chance to speak. When it's over Greene punches the key again, convinced that the exercise has provided no answers.

"Anybody?"

"If you don't mind." Julia clears her throat. "Ken and I took a quick getaway when the boys got older. We went to Memphis, Tennessee. We stayed at the Peabody Hotel. There was a blues festival. It was June. We stayed at the Peabody because we'd heard about the ducks." She quietly looks at each of us. "They have a Duck Master, who brings them down the elevator from the roof where they live, and they parade to a fountain in the middle of the lobby. This happens at eleven each day, when they come, and five each day, when they leave."

As I look around me I'm amazed to see how many mouths have dropped open at this revelation. Then I realize mine was, too. Could it possibly be this simple? Julia sits calmly as we all try to digest what we'd just heard. What a day of revelations. There is no spoofing this idea. No snide remarks or thoughts. After the day we'd all had there just wasn't anything about this suggestion that made it unlikely. Just the opposite.

Max laughs. "Goddamn."

It takes a few minutes for it all to sink in. We're getting someplace.

"How far is it to Memphis?" Greene asks. All eyes turn to Julia.

"Drive straight through, and you can do it in twenty hours," she says.

We let this sink in, too. A plan of action starts to form.

"Day after tomorrow," Max states. "Reid and I can drive it. I want to bring Jonny. The guy comes up with the damnedest things. We'll take his Mustang. And the arsenal."

"The rest of us will fly commercial," Yvette stakes out her spot before anyone can object.

"Let's get the travel arrangements in place. Where to stay," Julia adds.

"And where to meet up, that kind of thing," Greene chimes in. "Anything else?"

"Yeah," Max says, expression grim. "I'll call Brennan. He needs to have a CDC team at the Peabody."

"So we get there," I say. "What are we there for? What can we do?"

I'm looking at Max. He looks back, frowns, nods his head up and down, glances at Reid. Understanding.

"He's picking up the 'package'," he explains. "It must be the suitcase from the St. Lawrence. He sent it ahead, maybe in the trash hauler. Now he needs to get it back. He has some plan for dispersal. We need to get it from him before the next step happens." Max takes a breath. "We need to isolate him. Take him down. Protect the case no matter what. We'll identify him and follow until we can overpower him and safely obtain the case."

We all chew on that a little, more heads nod in agreement. Finally the silence is broken.

"Let's go," Reid says.

73

On the Road East

Wade Jennings throws the rest of his gear into the back of the pick-up. Gas cans and water bottles to be filled. Chests for food. Ammo canisters, a few automatic rifles. The clear blue sky stretches all around him, the mountaintop retreat so high and remote it seems like another world, a place to ride the wind. He calls to his younger brother, Vernon.

"Let's go, you asshole," He swings his bulk behind the wheel and pulls the door shut. "I want to get there in time to pleasure some of those women in West Memphis before we check out this Boris fuck."

Vernon's boyish face appears at the other door, hair sticking out, eyes too close, built like a bear.

"I thought he was the true light, the guy who figured out how we could keep more than fifty percent of what we take in. What's to check out? And anyway, what's wrong with our local whores? Ain't never heard you complainin'."

"You just never been no place nor done nothin'. I probably shouldn't spoil you for the local hookers. They suit you, fine. Leave the Arkansas ass to me. They'll be happier, and so will I."

"Go on and fuck yourself. We goin' or stayin'?"

"Goin'. Get in. We got a couple days travel ahead."

The pick-up slowly works its way around the rough spots in the rut filled, hard packed, dirt. They work their way down the mountain on roads no sane person would ever travel.

74

On The Road West

Sandwiches and water bottles fill the space behind the front seat of the Mustang. Couple of pillows and a blanket filled the backseat.

"What kind of support do you think he'll have?" Reid asks.

"Hard to say, especially if he's planning to use some of the militia assets." Max thinks for a moment. "I don't think he will, though. He still needs to control this thing. Everything he's done has been geared to keep the whole operation in his wheelhouse, nobody else's."

"Think that warehouse you and Jonny were in was the hub for his operatives?"

"Could be. We've hurt him. Gotta be down ten men."

"How will he adjust to that, Max?"

"He might not even know about the guys he sent to Big Moose. They didn't call to say they got wiped out, or that they succeeded. Could confuse and worry him, force him to make changes, mistakes."

"His confidence probably took a hit when you escaped," Reid adds.

"And beat the shit out of him," Jonny throws in from the driver's side.

Max smiles.

"What's Greene gonna' do?" Reid asks.

"He's flying down with the Manns and Julia. He'll do what he can. He's in a tough spot, not used to straying this far from the Agency."

"Why's he doing it?"

"Can't help himself. He has a finely honed concept of right and wrong." Max is quiet for a moment. "I don't know how far he'll stray, but he won't get in our way, may help with some interference."

"As long as he helps," Reid says and then turns his attention to Jonny. "What do you think of all this, Jonny? CIA, FBI."

Jonny smiles, never taking his eyes off the road. "My momma warned me about guys like you."

Max laughs, but watching Pennsylvania turn into Ohio, the rolling hills, the continuous string of semi's transporting food and materials, the small towns crowded into every nook and cranny, traffic everywhere, he can't help but wonder what kind of wasteland this could all turn into if Boris Sarnow is allowed to succeed. 'From sea to shining sea,' Jon from the CDC had told him. Max's jaw sets and his eyes harden. Reid notices this from the backseat. He knows what it means. They are going in, and they are coming out on top.

75

FBI, Albany, New York

"Hello, James. Did you get the files I sent over?"

Greene paced in front of his desk. He was dressed casually today, khaki pants, blue golf shirt, loafers. An overnight bag sat on the chair next to him.

James Ostermann is the US Attorney for the Northern District of New York, the lead guy for the governments non-intervention policy as regards Boris Sarnow. Greene had to leave for the airport shortly, but wanted to touch base, hopeful that Justice would decide to weigh in on this threat.

"Don't get pissed off, John, but did you come by this legally? It didn't come from a felon or rogue agents?"

"Search warrant signed by a real judge, James. We tried to get Judge Judy, but she was taping her show that day."

"Not that funny, John."

"What have we got, James?"

"Well." Ostermann paused and took a deep breath. "It's explosive. That's the only term I can think of. Apparently Dixon put this case together all on his own. A brilliant job. Seems he was worried about getting sidelined by his superiors.

"He must have been very close to action. The files are seemingly complete. It places this Russian, Sarnow, at the head of an international money laundering operation as well as being the brains behind criminal manipulation of international agricultural markets. Of course we have to verify most of the information referenced. The prosecutors have to decide the best way to proceed. The files, like I said, are very complete, though. I think we could be in a position to move on this by Christmas."

"Are you starting to like Sarnow for the terror threat I've told you about? Enough to take the handcuffs off and let the Agency move on it?"

"That's a whole different matter. We have a file that's not verified; no judge or jury has said this guy is guilty, or suspected of, anything. The political map as regards Boris Sarnow has not changed. I'll warn you again, Agent Greene, to respect those positions. We've suffered shit storms for this kind of thing before. It's not going to happen again. I hope we're clear on that?"

Greene had to smile to himself. 'None so blind.'

"OK James. Got to go." Greene didn't want to miss his flight to Memphis.

76

Albany Medical Center Hospital, Albany, New York

Eli Massry showed his credentials to the guard outside Jason Broner's hospital room. Broner was half sitting in his hospital bed. Semi-recumbent, due to the puncture wounds in his abdomen. IV lines went into his arm, a cannula provided extra oxygen, the pale green color of the tubes snaking around his neck and into his nose making Broner' pasty face look even more distressed. A comforting steadiness came from the beeps of the various monitors. Massry stood respectfully inside the door as the nurse fixed Broner's pillows, then nodded to Massry to come in.

"The detectives are downstairs," she told him. "Let the guard know when you and your client are ready for them."

Massry smiled a 'thank you' and approached the bed. Broner rolled his eyes in Massry's direction. If his face lacked blood, his eyes lacked life. He'd lost weight during his brief incarceration.

"Hello, Jason."

"I told you they'd get me," Broner accused. "I told you I was toast if you didn't get me out of there."

"Believe it or not, things may be looking up for you, Jason. If we're lucky."

"Why? What's happened?"

"You remember that group I told you about? The one that's going after Boris Sarnow?" Massry paused to allow Broner to catch up. "They may be getting close. They've already uncovered evidence that should make him a suspect."

"They said there's cops here to see me. Are they gonna' offer me a deal? Witness protection?"

"I don't know, Jason, but I think they're here to talk to you about the assault."

"I don't know fuck about the assault except that it was gonna' happen."

"Then that's what you tell them, Jason. Shall I call them up?"

Fendrick and Callahan appeared about five minutes later. Callahan looked like he didn't want to be there. Fendrick looked like he was ready to shoot somebody. Anybody.

"My client is still weak and under medication. Please keep your questions short and to the point."

"They killed my fuckin' nephew trying to get to this piece of shit. I'll ask my questions anyway I want," boomed Fendrick. Callahan was studying something on the floor.

"Excuse me, detective, but the man that did this was apprehended at the scene. You have dozens of witnesses to what happened, including the deputies present. My client really has nothing additional to offer."

"He knows who was behind this," sputtered a red faced Fendrick. "Just like he knows who hired him to kill Dixon."

Massry and Callahan stared at Fendrick.

"We're very sorry for your loss, detective. Your nephew was very brave. Undoubtedly he saved my client's life. We're very grateful."

Fendrick glared at Massry, at Broner, and stormed out of the room. Luckily, the air-cushioned door didn't slam, though he sure tried. Callahan looked up.

"He got that job for his nephew. The favorite uncle. A real cop. He'll never admit it, but he got the case wrong from the start. Feels responsible."

"Where is the inmate that did the stabbing?"

"Two floors up. Intensive care. The docs say he probably won't come out of the coma. The boys really did a job on him." Callahan shook his head, as if overcome by it all.

"Any information about him?" Massry asked.

"No, not really. No priors. He's new here. Waiting for word from Belarus. So far nothing."

"Has he family in Belarus?"

"Don't know," Callahan shrugged and followed his partner out the door.

77

Memphis, Tennessee

As arranged, we meet up at a Best Western just outside of town, near the airport. Max, Reid, and Jonny don't look any the worse for their marathon road trip. Greene seems despondent, Yvette and Julia determined. Murphy hard to read. I don't know what I feel. Was it a good thing that I witnessed Kenneth Dixon's murder? Otherwise this madman might be unhindered in his quest to destroy the United States. I just couldn't reconcile any way to view that man's murder as serendipitous. There would have been some other way to stop this. It would have fallen to someone else. That's what I wanted to believe. But there was nobody else. Absent the curious and roundabout way that this group came together, Boris would move unchallenged. But challenged he'd been.

"Today's the day," Max said. "How was your flight?"

"A little too quiet after all we've been through," I said.

"That's OK," he answered. "It'll heat up a little now."

Max went on to say they'd gotten in early and scoped the lobby of the Peabody.

"Jonny and I will stay out of sight. He'd recognize us. We can't tip our hand. Chance is he won't be expecting any opposition, so we should be able to surprise him."

"There's a balcony that offers a real good surveillance platform," Reid added. "I'll be up there with Julia and Yvette keeping an eye on everything that goes on below when the ducks show up."

Max looks at me. "I need you on the lobby floor. Pick him up and don't let him out of your sight. Follow him out. There's a lot of ways out of that lobby, but me, Jonny, Murphy and Greene figure we can cover it."

"We'll have positions across the street in each case, coffee shops, restaurants, like that," Murphy added.

Max hands me a small Glock to carry in my boot, just in case.

"Time to saddle up," Max smiles. To Reid he says, "Let's get your gear out of the Mustang's trunk."

We file out of the motel. The sky has grown ominous and the first large drops of rain have begun to fall. Yvette, Julia, Reid and me get into the rental car we picked up at the airport and head to downtown Memphis, wipers soon on high. Murphy and Greene go with Max and Jonny in the Mustang to set up at the Peabody exits.

Game on.

78

Peabody Hotel, Memphis, Tennessee

The Peabody Hotel is a Memphis landmark. It's been said that the Mississippi Delta begins in the lobby of the Peabody Hotel and ends on Catfish Row in Vicksburg. Compared to the great hotels of the world since it opened in 1869, and in spite of a brief closure in the 1970's, the Peabody represents the best of southern hospitality and grandeur. Over it's life it has hosted Presidents, Confederate Generals, plantation owners, gamblers, movie stars, and today will be a silent accomplice to an ongoing and unprecedented act of terrorism against the United States of America.

The Peabody takes up a whole city block, with wide boulevards taking traffic on one-way adventures on each side of the building. The Mississippi River and Beale Street are just a few minutes walk, as is the Desoto Bridge into Arkansas.

Victor opens the small door of his compartment and squeezes out between the two former spetsnaz in the front seats. They've parked at the back of the hotel, near where the loading docks are located and the garbage removed. High doors with large ramps allow the huge trucks into this underground Hades, where the lifeline for the hotel's supplies chugs along 24/7.

"Finally," Victor says, glancing at his watch. "An hour until we get into position. Vassaly, you're clear on what to do?" A nod from the passenger's seat.

"After your drop you go cover the street and the limo. I will have the package covered the whole time. Once the Boss has the case we cover him until he's back in the limo," Victor awaits the quick affirmative nods from both men. "I will join him, you will follow us over the bridge and continue west until you receive new instructions."

More nods, even a grunt from the driver. Satisfied, Victor retreats to his space for a liberal dose of fabric spray and deodorant, the next chapter in this odyssey about to begin.

79

The Peabody

The lobby of the Peabody was luxurious, epitomizing the South as it is today. Antebellum grace and hospitality mixed with the flow of today's economic patterns. If you had the price of admission, you got in. Well dressed ladies in pearls and diamonds enjoying afternoon tea didn't seem out of place with the young man in the baseball cap and the T-shirt that asked, 'Who the fuck is Mick Jagger?'.

The balance, or lack of it, was good for me. It helped me to fit in, hopefully not conspicuous as I surveyed the lobby, watching for the man who might be the key to Boris's plan of destruction. I'd gotten Boris' description from Mac and Jonny. Boris historically had stayed out of the limelight. Pictures of him were rare. No Facebook page for him. Max thought I might recognize the person dropping the case, that there seemed to be a pattern of an Eastern European ethnic pool working for Boris.

As I watched the people around me I realized what an eclectic mix travelled to Memphis these days. There were women in Burkas, men of Asian and Indian origin. Southerners and Northerners of every economic level. Europeans from Ireland and Great Britain. Fortunately, although the lobby was large by hotel standards these days, it was completely open, the ceiling rising above the mezzanine level, with the comfortable sofas, chairs and occasional tables all visible from where I sat. The decorative bar was at one end of the hall, with a Steinway piano playing itself at the other. The center of the room was graced with the world famous fountain in which the Peabody Ducks resided from 11am to 5 pm each day.

Shops lined the perimeter of the lobby opposite the registration desk and the concierge' counter. People wandered in out of Lansky's clothing shop, 'Clothiers to the King', where Elvis Presley famously was outfitted by Lansky himself. I prayed we deduced the meet accurately. As backup, Max, Murphy, and Jonny had taken up strategic positions outside the hotel. Jonny was in Hooters, Mac at T.G.I.F. Fridays, and Murphy in the breakfast place. Beale Street, world famous for music and musicians, was only a few blocks away. Greene stood in the lobby of an adjacent hotel. Posters proclaimed that BB King would be in town shortly, at his own club on Beale.

Movement by the entrance next to the coffee shop caught my eye. The man entering the lobby looked out of place, even for this well mixed group. A large man with heavy features, dark eyes, and an expressionless face. He towed a black suitcase on wheels, not out of place in this traveler's mecca. He approached the fringe of the crowd that had gathered for the parade. People of all ages lined up near the elevator the ducks would exit and lined the red carpet leading to the fountain. Folks with small children wedged their way to the front row, all with cameras or cell phones at the ready. Many of the onlookers were wearing ponchos, carrying umbrellas, or both. The colorful scene made the man in the drab suit more noticeable.

I glanced up to the railings around the mezzanine, where crowds had also gathered to watch the parade of the Peabody Ducks. I could make Reid out, a movie camera up to his eye.

I could feel my pulse rate going up. The man with the black suitcase towed it around the outskirts of those assembled in the lobby. I looked ahead to where the dark man seemed to be heading, but saw nothing of interest. Like many people in this Southern city, I was wearing a pair of elegant, if worn, cowboy boots. Unlike most, my right boot concealed the Glock, brought across country by Max in Jonny's red '65 Mustang. If necessary, I was to use that pistol to either hold Boris, or to take him down. It had sounded very straightforward when Max described how it would work. Stop him or shoot him.

The man circled the lobby, passed by the bar, where I was sitting, and was now standing next to a column across from Lansky's Menswear. He was looking toward the reservation desk on the other side of the room, near the exit leading to the garage and taxi pickup. I followed his gaze. There was a tall man in a tan raincoat carrying a golf umbrella standing on the stairs inside the door. The man was wearing a rain hat with the brim pulled down. I couldn't get a good look at the man's face, but I could see that he was the right height and build to be Boris. I saw this new man nod to the one next to the pillar. As I watched, the heavyset man in the dark suit put his hands in his pockets and headed out the hotel door to the streets of Memphis.

The black roller bag was standing next to the pillar, now unattended.

* * *

I was certain that it was Boris working his way from across the room through the crowd, and that he was headed for the bag standing next to the pillar about ten feet away from where I was sitting.

The crowd made it difficult to keep Boris in view as he casually moved towards Lansky's and the abandoned bag. A sudden thought struck me, the simplicity and clarity of it overpowering. I didn't have to follow or stop Boris at all. If I could just secure the case with the *puccinia* the Feds would have their proof. The country would be safe. They could pick Boris up at their leisure.

Boris worked his way past the reservation desk. Soon he would be passing around the outside of the bar, which would block him from my sight, but also block me from his. I jumped up and wedged between two large potted plants. Two steps later I had one hand on the bags telescopic handle. I didn't look back, but down the hallway to my right. The hallway to my left went past the elevator bank, and was blocked by the onlookers and the Peabody Ducks parade route. The exit straight ahead was the one taken by Boris's accomplice, and I didn't want to chance running into him.

"Drop it."

I froze. Standing in front of Lansky's shop a small man in a suit squared off at me. His hand was clearing his inside jacket pocket. I saw a pearl handle in that hand.

The shot drowned out the crowd noises. A hole appeared in the little man's forehead. The pink spray covered Lansky's window for a second, then the man fell backward and through the glass, which shattered unto the marble floor. The crowd went mad, women and children screaming, men shouting, the ducks panicking and making an unholy racket of their own.

Reid, hurt arm and all had made that shot from the mezzanine with a handgun.

Everyone was on the deck now, scrambling for the exits. I glanced quickly at the end of the bar and saw Boris standing with his umbrella pointed at me. I jumped behind the pillar as another blast panicked the crowd and took out Lansky's other display window. I picked the case up, held it across my chest, and took off in a sprint towards my exit, running broken field around bodies, sometimes over them. The corridor seemed to go on forever, the noise rising as the terror spread, screams and profanity combining into one terrifying ululation. I forced my way down the steps guarded by the large bronze dogs and joined the scrum at the revolving doors. The suitcase across my chest made it impossible to use my arms and I wound up jammed inside the doorframe, unable to move, watching the crowd surge as the bottleneck got worse. I also caught sight of Boris advancing with difficulty along the perimeter. Still advancing, while I was stopped dead.

"Get off my fucking foot," screamed a young woman just ahead of me.

"Shut the fuck up," a man with spittle flying from his mouth shot back.

"Everyone move this way so the door opens," bellowed a construction worker almost at the exit.

People leaned their weight in the direction he pointed. The few precious inches gained moved the door just enough, and in the midst of all the chaos and panic a bunch of people tumbled out onto the wet sidewalk, and then another bunch.

I ran down the street to my right, toward Beale. A quick look back and I saw Boris, in the street now, headed towards me. The umbrella was cradled in Boris' left arm. He was pulling his right hand from inside his raincoat. I could see the pistol. The rainsquall had driven the escaping crowd the other way, flooding the intersection and seeking shelter in the hotels and restaurants scattered up the street. The few cars passing by had windshield wipers on high, and windows fogged from the downpour. The next cross street was too far. I'd never make it. There was one opening ahead, part of the hotel.

The open bay doors revealed trucks parked in an expansive area, and the smell that assailed my nostrils told me this was where the Peabody's garbage accumulated.

"Hey! You can't come in here."

I saw a man in coveralls over by one of the trucks start towards me.

"Call the cops," I yelled. "There's a man with a gun."

The man changed course and disappeared behind one of the trucks. He'd been on the other side of the huge garage. I couldn't follow him. Not enough time. I spotted a couple of beat up metal doors up some stairs just down the bay. I ran for them.

I took the stairs two at a time. Pulled on the first door. Locked. A desperate look back to the street. No sign of Boris. The second door had a latch handle. The handle turned and I leapt through, pulling the door closed behind me. I set the case down and leaned against the wall with my hands on my knees, trying to catch my breath, straining to hear. It only took a couple of breaths before I was once again in full survival mode. I looked around.

There was one ceiling light, a bulb encased in a metal jacket, and a narrow stairway going down. As I went down the stairs I could hear the sound of machinery somewhere in the bowels of the building, a distant humming. At the bottom of the stairs a narrow tunnel went off to the left. Another jacketed light shown dimly about twenty feet away, a number of puddles reflected the dim light.

I clutched the bag and went on. Skirting one of the puddles I heard the sound of the metal door being pulled open. To my horror I then heard it as it closed. Then footsteps.

I hurried the length of the tunnel like corridor to where it turned right. I looked quickly behind me and thought I could just make out a foot and leg appear near the bottom of the stairs. I turned the corner and saw that the hallway I was in intersected another corridor ten feet ahead of me. Still taking care with the puddles and the noise I ran to the junction, deciding to go right, maybe farther into the building, to a way up, to escape.

★ ★ ★

"Shit."

The metal door was locked. Barred from the other side from what I could see. I was in a small alcove just off the tunnel after I'd made the choice to go right, deeper into the building. As I crouched against the immovable door I thought I could feel air moving down the corridor behind me. I couldn't help but think I should have gone left.

Stop and think. Breathe, in, out. I still had the Glock.

Close to the floor, I peered cautiously around the edge of the alcove and could make out a shadow moving along the wall on my side of the hallway. The figure was crouched and moving steadily towards me, close to the wall, a small target. I did my best to steady my shaking hand by using my other hand to brace it against the masonry. I aimed down the barrel at the dark shape in front of me and slowly applied pressure to the trigger, wondering if Boris was doing the same thing.

The gunshot was deafening in those close quarters, the bullet ricocheting down the hall. Even as he crouched at the sound of the gunfire Boris raised his arm and released a volley from what must have been a shotgun. I ducked back into the alcove with bricks chipping and bullets hitting all around me, placing the case where my body offered some protection. I pointed my gun around the corner and fired three times. There was another loud blast. It lit up the tunnel and deafened me, with pellets flattening themselves on the walls all around me.

I leaned out to see if that was a farewell salvo only to see Boris, half erect and coming directly at me, a weapon in each hand. I rolled into the damp corridor, supporting the glock with both hands, counting to slow my breathing and steady my hands. I fired two rounds. One caught Boris in the shoulder, half turning him around, he dropped his pistol. The other seemed to get him in the abdomen. He dropped the shotgun-cum-umbrella and clutched his gut with that hand.

Boris turned and ran as best he could back down the passageway. After a few seconds I scrambled to my feet and chased after him. He ran past the entryway that I had come through and continued down the corridor. I rounded a bend and just caught sight of him opening a rusty steel gate. I rushed toward him. Boris stepped through as soon as the opening allowed, and shoved the gate closed. I got to the gate a second later, only to find that there had been a clasp and lock hanging on the gate, apparently open. Now closed and locked.

There was a street crossing right in front of the gate Boris had exited. Even if I had bullets left I couldn't take a chance on hitting the people lined up on the other side of the street, waiting to cross. Boris realized this, stopping in the downpour and turning so that I could see his face. I saw hate and triumph as Boris, still holding his side with one hand, pointed at me. He made a slicing motion across his neck. Chills went down my spine and I felt a hollowness in my gut.

As Boris turned to continue to the other side of the street I saw people on the curb raising their hands to their mouths, eyes opening wide, looking down the street at something the concrete walls kept me from seeing and the pounding rain kept me from hearing

Then I heard the sound of a racing engine. The street where Boris was crossing was suddenly filled with bright red color. The red '65 Mustang with the steel reinforced grill was still accelerating as it made contact with the Boss.

I felt sick as I watched the car hit. Then he was gone, out of my field of vision. He'd gone airborne at impact, like a rag doll, over the hood and roof of the Mustang and on down the road. I heard the car race around a corner, and it was gone. The crowd disappeared toward where the ragdoll of a body must've landed. In front of me were Boris' shoes, empty now, gently rocking on the wet road where he'd been struck. My knees gave out and I slumped forward, the gate all that was holding me up.

* * *

Passing the corridor I'd come through a lifetime ago I continued and retrieved the suitcase. My knees were weak, sweat dripped from my face. I headed back and heard footsteps in the outer corridor. They were moving slowly. I'd thought to retrieve the pistol Boris had dropped, but had no idea if there was any ammo left in it. First I took a cautious look around the paint chipped doorframe. Crouched low, pistol held in front of him, Jonny crept along the passageway.

"Jonny," I called to him. Jonny froze in place.

"You OK?"

"Yeah, I am now."

I emerged from the doorway, suitcase in hand.

"Where's Boris? We spotted you running out of the hotel, Boris chasing you. I followed, but took the wrong door upstairs, that's why it took me so long to get here. Max took my car and drove to the other side, in case you got back out on the street."

"Boris got out of here. Max caught up with him." Jonny raised an eyebrow. "He ran him down with your car, I don't think there'll be much left of him."

Jonny pursed his lips and furrowed his brow. I wondered if he was calculating the potential damage to his Mustang.

"That's what happens when you let somebody borrow your car. Let's get out of here. He may still have friends out on the street. Good thing about going the wrong way, I found a route back into the main part of the hotel. We should get there, quick. Avoid the cops."

* * *

Jonny led me past the concierge's desk. The lobby was surprisingly calm. On the other side I could see someone was sweeping up the glass outside of Lansky's. Someone was also zipping up a black body bag. There were police and paramedics hanging around, tending the folks injured in the stampede. No sign of the drake and the four hens. We slipped into a small office off the unloading area at the back. The first thing I was aware of was Yvette running up and throwing her arms around me, sobbing with relief. Julia was right next to her, as was Reid.

"We couldn't tell where you went from our spot on the rail," Julia explained. Reid looked relieved.

"Nice shot, I never even noticed him there," I said. He smiled.

"I see you still have the bag. How did you lose Boris?"

I heard sirens and took a quick look into the lobby. Cops and paramedics were on their cells.

"Those first responders are going to find a seriously injured, or more likely, dead, Boris. A hit and run. They'll also find two gunshot wounds in him. We need to get this bag to the right people and get out of here."

Murphy walked in. He opened his cell phone and made a

prearranged call. After about twenty seconds he flipped the phone closed.

"CDC is pulling up outside. They'll take the bag and all of us to a charter flight to DC. There's a side door we can go out."

* * *

We stood inside the Peabody, watching through a doorway leading to the covered area where limos and cabs dropped off and picked up their fares. There were three large Chevy Suburbans, dark blue, waiting at the curb. Reid had his hand on his pistol while we watched Murphy approach the middle vehicle. The driver's side window came down and IDs were exchanged and checked. Reid turned and gestured for us to come, quickly, which we did. The six of us crowded into the SUV, which swallowed us up with room to spare. I still carried the black suitcase.

The convoy pulled out of the hotels parking area and onto the main street. As we passed a cross street I saw the flashing lights of the emergency vehicles. There was a form in the street with a white shroud covering it. I wondered if I would be able to relax now.

The two men in the front of the SUV I was in didn't seem too inclined to chat.

"Where are we going," I demanded, surprised at the force of my own voice.

"The airport," said the man in the passengers seat, half turning. "We have four seats booked and will take off shortly after we get on board."

"What about the rest of us?"

"Max will be waiting at the airport," Murphy answered. "I'll go with Jonny and Reid and drive back. Max will fly with you and the ladies."

"Won't they be looking for the car involved in the hit and run?"

Reid answered, a wry smile on his face. "Eyewitnesses, notoriously unreliable though they sometimes are, have accurately described a late model, cherry apple red, Chevy Camaro as the car involved in the accident. The victim has not been identified. No personal effects will be recovered from the body."

The twenty minute ride to the airport was quiet. I was spent.

I went over it again and again. Boris was dead. The case with the deadly spores was on the floor between my knees. The government was apparently willing to get involved, finally. Justice had been done.

The three SUVs drove to the General Aviation part of the airport, to a hanger where a small jet was waiting.

"Well look at that," said Jonny. I followed his gaze to the '65 Mustang, a hundred feet from the plane, Max behind the wheel.

"Doesn't look bad," I said, but Jonny was already out of his seatbelt and half out of the car.

As I walked to the plane I watched Jonny give the car a quick examination. Max's head was nodding up and down, assuring Jonny it still handled well. When Jonny declared the car fit for travel Max clapped him on the shoulder and jogged to the plane. Within fifteen minutes we were airborne.

After an hour and a half the jet made a smooth landing at a small airfield outside of Washington. Three more dark blue Suburbans collected us for the forty minute drive to CIA headquarters. We were guided to a secure area and left to wait. After ten more minutes a large man in a lab coat, accompanied by what appeared to be high ranking CIA people, finally relieved me of the suitcase.

80

Epilogue

The day was cold but clear, with the autumn sunlight sparkling off the river. The Adirondacks were absent their colorful foliage now.

Yvette was at the stove putting the finishing touches on the Thanksgiving day dinner. The fireplace was roaring and the air inside the cabin was full of warmth and wonderful smells from the turkey and fixings. I'd added a couple of extensions to the table in order for everyone to fit. Reid and Murphy were out on the deck sampling the Power's whiskey. Julia sat with me, the conversation light as we watched Yvette's preparations and waited for Max to arrive. Jonny was invited but probably not going to show. I started when the newly installed landline rang and rushed to answer it.

"Mr. Mann," said the familiar voice.

"Agent Greene. Happy Thanksgiving."

"Same to you, sir. I thought it would be a good time to call and tie up any lose ends from Memphis."

I straightened and took a breath. As time passed I thought we might never hear anymore about it. The online newspapers had offered nothing – other than the murder in the lobby of the Peabody, Lansky's window being destroyed, and one of the ducks having been trampled.

"What have you got?"

"We're still investigating, after all we've got the CIA, FBI, and CDC all jockeying to figure out what happened and take the credit if anything did, but we have some preliminary findings I'd like to share with you."

"Did you say 'If anything did'?"

"Yes, Mr. Mann. It seems unclear. You see, the suitcase you gave us contained nothing that could be harmful to humans or plants."

"What?"

"That's right. Also, the victim of the hit and run in Memphis has not yet been identified. We think he was an illegal engaged in criminal activity, possibly killed by a business associate worried about competition."

"Greene, we both know that was Boris Sarnow that died on that street, and we know what he had planned."

"According to Boris's investment office he's alive and well. Currently on an extended business trip to Asia, where he's looking into relocating his office. They also said that no further details would be forthcoming." Greene breathed a sigh of finality.

"Dinners ready in ten minutes," Yvette called from the stove as I hung up.

Reid and Murphy came in. Reid took one look at me and started laughing.

"What's so funny?" I demanded.

"From the look on your face you just got off the phone with Greene. Right?"

"How do you know that?"

He laughed some more. Even Murphy had a grin on his face.

"We're dealing with the Government here. Never paying attention, but always right. Especially retrospectively."

"So what's the truth then?" We all looked to the front of the cabin as we heard footsteps on the porch. Max walked in with a big smile that froze on his face as he looked at me. He looked at Reid.

"Greene?"

"Yeah," Reid shook his head, the smile still there.

"Yvette," Max said. "Any chance of a couple more minutes before dinner is served?"

"Can do," she said, looking at each of us in turn.

We sat. Max looked each of us over, like a grandfather getting ready to tell the grandchildren what was in the will.

"It was him, alright," Max said. "They aren't going to admit to anything at the government level that would make them look like they were asleep at the wheel while a terrorist plot was happening."

"They know he's dead, too," Reid added.

"They also know he was the boss of the operation, and the financial genius behind the money laundering?" Julia asked.

Max nodded a silent 'yes'.

"The Feds have quietly seized the assets of Sarnow's management company," Max added. "His client's can't get to their money, Uncle Sam has it now, and they are pissed off."

"A big win," Murphy added, "stopping him and breaking the back of a money laundering operation with a world wide reach."

"Yeah," I said, "but nothing there they can take credit for, so they let it ride?"

"Their big success," Max said, "was the Russian's bio-terror weapon becoming their bio-terror weapon."

Julia was helping Yvette bring the feast to the table.

"They try to pretend there was no plot, no conspiracy," Max said as she placed a large platter full of turkey on the table next to him. "But Eli Massry was still able to make them back off the murder charge against Broner, or deal with embarrassing disclosures in court. Massry cornered the government into a plea bargain for his client. Manslaughter, twenty years, eligible for parole in ten."

"Enough business," Yvette hoisted her glass of wine. "It sounds to me like we can find a few things to be thankful for this Thanksgiving that don't involve Boris Sarnow."

I smiled at her, and at the others around the table, as they all joined in the toast.

The landline rang. We let it.

THE END

10005570R00133

Made in the USA
Lexington, KY
17 September 2018